"Are you not afraid of reaching a stage of inebriation I might be tempted to take advantage of?" he asked cocking one dark brow up.

"No. As you have reminded me several times earlier tonight—there is not anything else you could do with me you have not already done."

"What a little innocent you are, Chloe." He circled the table and took the flask and pulled her up from the chair. "I've thought a lot about you these past few months. Didn't want to. But did." He wrapped his arms around her and nuzzled her neck.

She breathed in the butterscotch whiskey and sandalwood smell she associated with him. Wanting to see if there was truth in his eyes, she pushed against his chest, locking her arms to study his face. Could she believe him?

"Tell me you want to kiss me too," he whispered.

Inch by inch she moved in, surrendering equal distance. Finally, their lips met as if no time had passed between them—a continuation of their night together a few months before. She could taste the heavy sweetness of the whiskey they had drunk, smell its heady scent, but it was his mouth, his touch that made her dizzy with desire.

Praise for Joy Allyson

"Joy Allyson's debut novel will have you turning pages from the start. When Chloe and Pen first meet more than whiskey wars are at play. *WHISKEY LOVE* has the perfect blend—a headstrong heroine, a swoon-worthy hero with a heart, and a gilded treasure trove of rapscallion characters. Irresistible!"

~*Kim Turner, author of*
The McCades of Cheyenne series

Whiskey Love

by

Joy Allyson

Happy Reading,
Joy Allyson

This is a work of fiction. Names, characters, places, and incidents are either the product of the author's imagination or are used fictitiously, and any resemblance to actual persons living or dead, business establishments, events, or locales, is entirely coincidental.

Whiskey Love

COPYRIGHT © 2022 by Joy Allyson

All rights reserved. No part of this book may be used or reproduced in any manner whatsoever without written permission of the author or The Wild Rose Press, Inc. except in the case of brief quotations embodied in critical articles or reviews.
Contact Information: info@thewildrosepress.com

Cover Art by *Diana Carlile*

The Wild Rose Press, Inc.
PO Box 708
Adams Basin, NY 14410-0708
Visit us at www.thewildrosepress.com

Publishing History
First Edition, 2022
Trade Paperback ISBN 978-1-5092-4191-0
Digital ISBN 978-1-5092-4192-7

Published in the United States of America

Dedication

To my husband, Hal,
and our two daughters Wren and Ashley
for always loving and encouraging me.
And to lifelong friend, Karen Ford,
who insisted—"Whiskey stories are the best!"

Acknowledgments

Many thanks to my editor Judi Mobley for her fantastic editing and for finding multiple ways to ask for "more."

Chapter One

Oak Hollow, Tennessee Late September 1892

"Maggie, who's that man staring at me?"

"Every man in this room is staring at you, Chloe." Her cousin paused mid-step. "Which one do you mean?"

"The one in the brown suit over by the door. Standing next to Milo," Chloe answered as the two descended the giant staircase of her family's Victorian Queen Anne style home. She stopped on the bottom step, still clasping the mahogany banister. Peering up to the turret tower on the third floor, she wished she could flee back up the stairs and barricade herself inside until everyone left.

"Oh, that's Pen Kittrell."

"Of Penland Kittrell Distillery?"

"The same."

"But he's too young." Chloe Tanner stood looking through the doorway to the parlor, undaunted by his perusal. *And way too handsome.* She toyed with the top button of her dress. Her pulse throbbed in her throat. His chiseled face, straight nose, and sweeping black lashes contrasted with a strong jawline. All belying her belief that attractiveness could ever project raw power. A flicker of a quizzical look betrayed his half smile hovering on his mustached lips. His dark brows rose then lowered down over intelligent—or were they amused—eyes.

Old Man Kittrell was at least eighty when he died. He had one son. And three wives. No other children. The man had an awful reputation. If there were any other offspring, indeed the entire county would know. This man had to be near her brother's age, around thirty. His black hair and bronze complexion confirmed the rumor of the Kittrells having Cherokee blood. Perhaps some Melungeon too, based on those turquoise eyes staring back at her. No matter their mixed blood, little doubt about it, the Kittrells produced the purest rye whiskey around. No equal there. But it was their signature sour mash whiskey, with its incredibly smooth finish, that kept them as Tanner's chief competitor.

He returned her stare, scrutinizing her from her head down to her toes, then up again—stopping where most men wondered if she stuffed her high-neck silk-and-lace bodice with padding—or in his case looked as if he knew every inch of her was real.

"What's he doing here? He wasn't at visitation last night or the funeral this morning?"

Her cousin shook her head. People clustered in groups throughout the front rooms of the house, staring at her and Maggie like they'd grown horns or tails. This collection of men wearing bowler hats and diamond stick pins, so different from the mourners who paid respects this morning.

Was Penland Kittrell like these parasites just waiting for the reading of her grandfather's will to see if they could gain control of Tom Tanner's Tennessee Whiskey? *I'd say it's obvious. Wants to eyewitness the demise of the competition.* Maybe not fair. He and Noah were sure to have known each other.

After the burial this morning, Milo Knox, the company's foreman, warned her to be prepared for New York paper reporters. Her aging black foreman came from a family of sharecroppers in the neighboring county who provided corn and workers for the distillery and looked after Tanner's as far back as she could remember. "No disrespect intended. To them, it's the summer's most sensational news story. Dying to cover it firsthand. I can see the headline now, 'Tom Tanner Distillery, the country's most famous whiskey maker, going to the one and only heir. A nineteen-year-old and a female to boot!' Be ready," he said patting her back.

"I'll be ready."

Pen Kittrell bent his head and spoke to Milo. Confident in demeanor, tall and broad shouldered, he was lean but appeared so coiled of energy the room just contained him. Hardly an even playing field, she determined, weighing her major rival. Her foreman nodded his head as they both glanced her way.

"He's coming over here now." She tightened her fists, bewildered when heat flushed through her body. *No sir, I won't let you or anyone else have my company.*

"Got to go." Her cousin kissed her on the cheek when her mother joined them. "We have a telephone now. Call if you need me."

Botheration, Jed Sanders, the general manager for Tom Tanner Distillery for four long years, slithered over and placed a possessive arm about her waist. Well, he could do that to her mother, but she wasn't having any of it.

"Mrs. Tanner, Miss Tanner," Milo said. "May I introduce Penland Kittrell to you?"

Chloe stepped out of Sanders' grasp and took Pen's hand. A gesture under the circumstances she did not have to extend. His clasp, comfortable in hers, was rough and calloused. *He works with his hands*. The thought surprised her.

She squinted upward at him for a better look. The few men she'd met before who were this handsome possessed smooth manicured hands. Not that she had been around many attractive young men in their twenties and thirties. But there was the day when her best friend's father took them to the Boston Racetracks unbeknownst to her aunt. He whisked them up to the owner's suite where plenty of touching took place during the afternoon as dapper young men pulled and stroked their hands across and into hers.

"I want to offer my sincere condolences," Pen said in a slow, deep drawl. So different than the men from Boston and New York whose fast nasal clips she was used to hearing.

"I know Pen, of course." Her mother tendered her hand. "I don't think I've seen this many members of the press since the time you and Noah got lost in that cave. You were just a baby, Chloe," she said glancing at her daughter, before turning back to Pen. "It took almost two full days to rescue you both, didn't it?"

"Yes, ma'am," Pen answered with an almost imperceptible shudder.

"Regina, we need to go in and take our seats so the attorneys can begin." Sanders looped his arm around her mother and guided her into the library. Pen nodded and stepped aside. Chloe entered the room choosing one of the three front chairs, the one next to the aisle and next to her mother and as far away as possible from her general manager.

Her back ramrod stiff, staring straight ahead, she felt a sensation. Pen Kittrell's presence, like a breath of summer's breeze on her neck. She glanced over her shoulder, noticing him out of the corner of her eye. He stood in the back of the room and nodded in acknowledgment, compelling her to turn around. Why was he still here?

"Thank you, everyone, for agreeing to stay this afternoon and allowing us to move along with our proceedings. And I want to express my thanks to Mrs. Tanner for opening her home on our firm's behalf in these unquestionably trying times." The senior attorney bowed, then sat between his partners at the table placed in front of the assembled group.

"Indeed, these are uncommon times," he continued. "We mourn the passing of our long-time proprietor Thomas Lewis Tanner the third. And we can thank God for delivering his grandson from a sure ocean grave so we could have a proper Christian burial and provide some closure for the family. I cannot recall in the fifty years of our law partnership ever losing the owner and the next in line in a simultaneous accident."

"Ohh." Chloe's mother cried into Sanders' shoulder.

Had it been just a month? Thirty days since word reached them that the *Athenian* was struck by another ocean liner a mere three miles out to sea in an unexplainable collision. There were no survivors from the sunken ship. Then a telegram arrived informing her mother that a body found washed onshore was identified as none other than her older brother, Noah Tanner, the lone one recovered from the wreck.

Just like that, she lost her only sibling and grandfather. A telegram was dispatched to Boston, and Chloe boarded the train along with her aunt whom she had lived with since age eleven, for the long trip back to her family's home in Oak Hollow, Tennessee.

"In the year of our Lord, 1892…" Half listening to the attorney drone on, she watched prisms of light steal inside the stained-glass transom windows, Father's single concession to Mother when designing the house. The refracted rays rested on the old globe alongside, where she and Grandpa had sat studying together. She closed her eyes to stay the tears threatening to fall.

He encouraged her to spin and spin, stopping at random and pointing out another spot on the earth where Tom Tanner's Tennessee Whiskey was sold. Markets ranging from San Francisco to New York, London, Paris, St. Petersburg, Singapore, across the South Pacific to the southern hemisphere could be traced.

Every summer, after moving away, for three glorious months her grandfather took her under his wing and provided her more love and nourishment than from anyone else in the family. Life within the Tanner household had been harsh. Her mother lost at least two babies between Noah's birth and hers if you counted the little headstones in the graveyard where they held the service this morning. And then to lose her father too. Under ghastly circumstances. Circumstances which led to her being sent to live with her aunt in the east. Chloe patted her mother's hand. Sometimes it was not hard to understand why her mother sought out the companionship of Jed Sanders. A man who for whatever reason made her skin crawl.

The lawyer continued reading from Grandfather's will. Everything was left to her. Of course, she was named as descendant. No names. Had her brother even had a will? He was unmarried, just turned thirty. It wouldn't have mattered, the attorneys told them. Noah never lived to inherit.

"My sterling silver scales presented by Queen Victoria's daughter Princess Alexandra, at the Royal Jubilee Exhibition"—Chloe sat up at the attorney's inflection change—"I will to Penland Kittrell." She forced herself not to turn and watch his reaction. So that is why he was here. *I'd love to ask Grandpa why he made such a bequest. Interesting.* Chairs scuffled across the oak floors as the lead attorney folded the papers, glanced at his gold pocket watch, and drew the proceedings to a close.

"Won't you come with me, Chloe, to the plant office? You can help me pack the scale for Pen to take home," Milo asked, tapping her on her shoulder.

"Yes."

Anything to remove herself from the over-emotional atmosphere swirling around the house and the heavy scent wafting from the flower arrangements. Hurrying outdoors without any goodbyes or looking back, she rushed down the beaten path toward the distillery.

Breathing in the autumn air, she welcomed the fresh puffs blowing on her cheeks. Cooler in the hollow and much chillier once the sun dropped in the late afternoon, perfect conditions for aging the three hundred barrels of whiskey racked in their warehouse.

A squirrel chasing hickory nuts zigzagged in front of her before scurrying across the lawn. Crabapple tree leaves were already tinting red for fall. This would be the first September spent at her family's home in over a decade. Sighing, she wished she had time to enjoy the change of seasons. However, that did not fit with any of her plans.

She scampered to the base of the hill where Tanner House stood, the single rise in elevation of the one hundred acres of Tanner land. It was a quick race past the barn and stables until she reached the small footbridge crossing to the distillery. The family mansion's ornate shingles, mansard roof, domes, spires, and lacy friezes presented a direct contrast to the rugged sprawling work complex.

Unlike the whiskey made inside, the distillery's two-story exterior was simple and plain. Horizontal brown-stained, hand-hewn cedar logs, with notched ends interlocking stretched for fifty yards. Three cupolas crowned the vaulted roof allowing ventilation. Inside, solid milled tongue and groove walls of cedar and oak supported by timber beams housed the offices, the drying rooms, the mash turns, the ever-important copper still, spirit safes, and waiting barrels. From her vantage point, she made out the new rick house behind the main structure that stored the barreled whiskey.

The stream located behind the distillery gurgled louder and louder, plunging the pure spring water down to the bedrock limestone below. The naturally filtered water provided the source for both the Tanners' and Kittrells' whiskies. The finest distilled in all the Americas. Recalling Milo's slow pace, she halted midway on the bridge and turned to wait for him.

Penland Kittrell was coming with him. Good, she thought, watching the two men advance. She had hoped against hope he would. Her plan, if she chose to pursue it, left no time for indecision. It had to work. And this was her best opportunity. Pen walked at a comfortable gait beside her limping plant foreman. He leaned close to her most trusted employee's head full of grizzled hair, laughing at something he said. Once they reached her, Pen lifted his broad-brimmed hat and smiled. Oh, yes, the jittery feeling gave way when gazing up into his handsome face. A sudden blush crept into her cheeks along with a pang of guilt, the imaginings of what she would like to do with him. The sparkle in his eyes hinted he read her mind.

"Very nice of you to do this. You could have mailed it to me," he said replacing his hat without taking his eyes off her.

Oh, bother. Was this man always this maddening? She turned and walked on.

"You're staying tonight," Milo informed him. "It'd take you too long to ride back to the other side of the split. Got you bunking in the bachelor quarters. Sorry, we chucked you in with the New York fellow," he guffawed. "The scale you inherited will give you two a bit to discuss. I'm sure he'll want to see it."

Chloe waited by the door, then the trio entered the deserted distillery. No employees bustling about their work today. They walked upstairs in the quiet to her grandfather's office. There, resting behind his desk below the wood-carved quotation of Mark Twain's, "Too much of anything is bad, but too much good whiskey is barely enough," was the scale. Placed alongside was the trophy from the 1876 Centennial

Exposition held in Philadelphia. Both awards put Tom Tanner's Number Five on the whiskey connoisseur's map. The objects were permanent fixtures in the room as far back as Chloe could remember along with two original bottles of Tom Tanner's Tennessee Whiskey. Bottles which made the distillery's distribution reach possible because her family was one of the first to sell whiskey in bottles rather than by the jug or the barrel.

"I think I gathered why he wanted you to have this. I've heard more than once your great-grandfather happened to be the reason we entered the competition," Milo revealed.

"You two head over to the tasting room, while I pack this up."

She agreed, knowing her foreman suggested this for her benefit. To remain in Grandpa's office would be too heart-rending.

"Here you go. Sustenance," Milo said returning a few minutes later. He placed two shot glasses on the round table after pouring whiskey into thumbnail glass tumblers from the tasting counter.

Both took their drinks. Chloe banged hers down on the table after her first sip. "Milo, what's this? You gave me Lady's Luck," she pouted. Pen reached over and raised her tumbler to his nose, then tasted the remains.

"She's right, Milo." He glanced over at her. Was he calculating her expertise on discerning the difference between his drink and hers? He lifted both shot glasses. "Let's have a refill. Of the good stuff, no less. I'd say she deserves it, after all she's been through."

Milo acquiesced and took the stopper out of Number Five from the counter and ambled back, pouring each another dram. After finishing the second drink, she unbuttoned the top button of her black silk dress and tossed her head, shaking her black slate earrings, her solitary mourning jewelry.

"Give him a tour while I try to find packing material for the scale. You came on horseback, right?" Milo confirmed before shuffling off.

Pen's forehead wrinkled. "Still can't believe the one person the Yankees shot when they trooped through here was a black man."

"Well, he was trying to keep them from setting fire to our distillery. I grew up at his knee with him entertaining me and the other distillery kids with the story. He loved to recount when the marauders came through stealing everything they could and burning the rest, Grandpa said they could have the whiskey, but if they destroyed the copper still, that'd be the end of us. He and Milo and the organist from the Methodist church in Nolensville, the Yankees had just burned it to the ground, held them off for three days. Did you know that? Till Milo snuck a wagon packed with whiskey barrels down to the river and dumped it, knowing they'd chase after it. Worked like a charm."

" 'Cept he still has a bullet fragment in his leg. Damn if I'd go on working for thirty years after that."

"He said he was lucky to be alive. We know we're lucky he stayed."

Pen stood close. The trouser leg of his tailor-cut suit touched her skirt. He angled his head toward her, searching her eyes, then smiled again. His teeth were so white, and his mustache trimmed neat, not bushy like so many of the mountain men about. What would it be like to kiss him? Not that she had any experience to compare him with. No way she could count the time Bartholomew Overby grabbed her in the cloakroom at Miss Lanning's dance school and pressed his lips on hers.

"Let's go downstairs and walk through where they fill the barrels," she suggested. Before they descended the stairs, Chloe stopped and leaned on the banister overlooking the distillery below. The scene never failed to conjure a rush of pride in her. "I always loved this view."

Pen joined her, placing his hands on the rail beside hers. Their little fingers touched. Chloe lifted hers then lowered it, brushing hers against his. Almost like a caress.

She bent over the railing before rocking back and tossing her head. "You know, women's influence with Tanner Whiskey is not new. It was my great-great-grandmother's recipe that my great-grandpa brought over from Scotland to make our whiskey."

"Not surprising," he said, turning and facing her again.

"As a Tanner, I had to learn the whiskey business from the ground up. My first job was to show the farmers where to take the grain we bought. I graduated from sweeping the charcoal spillage around the filtering vat to watching the thermometers on the mash tanks."

"When did you first start tasting?"

"When I was sixteen."

"Not just old-timers believe a woman's palate is more refined than men's."

"I can tell the difference between sassafras and gingerroot in a blind taste test any day of the week."

Pen nodded, shifting his weight leaning closer. "I

have to be honest. I've walked through every inch of your distillery. I worked here one summer."

"No, you couldn't have, or when? I've been here every summer, even after I moved away."

"It was five years ago, right before my father died. It would have been in '88."

She grimaced. "The spring I broke my arm. Right before I was to leave, I got thrown from a horse. I'd forgotten." She rubbed her wrist to her elbow. "I didn't get to come that year. Why did you work here?"

"Your grandfather calculated it'd be useful for both of our companies if we shared some labor methods. Noah worked at Kittrell's, and I came here."

"Did it work?"

"Some might say so. The experience gave me a chance to get to know your grandpa. A truly great man."

She felt her eyes glisten. "Yes, he was." Changing the subject, she asked how well he knew her brother.

"We were in the same class at Fortress Heights. Boarded the same train every term and came back together for four years.

"Did you like going to a military school?"

"Not at all."

"Sometime I'll have to tell you about the female academy I attended in Boston. It's surprising what you can get away with using a few la de das," she said in an exaggerated southern accent. They walked past the vessels swiveling the mash to the large washback tanks, where yeast was added, and fermentation turned sugar into alcohol.

"We built a new rick house next door a year ago when we ran out of space inside here for storing the whiskey casks," she said as they strolled among empty stacked barrels waiting to be filled.

"The Tanners claim it was divine providence that our forebears settled in this part of the country, more like serendipity. Our happy coincidence—since our whiskeys like nothing better than our sweltering summers and crisp winters to mature. Grandpa would always remind me when I'd complain about burning up or freezing to death. Best place on earth to not lose more than our 'Angel's Share' he'd say."

She walked him by the giant twelve-foot-high oak barrel built for promotion purposes located at the lower end of the factory. "White oak, the finest wood for aging whiskey." Circling the cask she gave it a reverential stroke, sliding her hand over the drum. "Don't you think so?" Their hands touched when Pen smoothed his hand over the expansive barrel, pausing over hers when his fingers brushed her hand.

She twisted around, placing herself in front of him, raising up on the tips of her toes and pressing her body into his, then curled her arms about his neck, and kissed him. For a frozen instant, his lips remained unmoving beneath hers. Then, as if floodgates opened, he wrapped his arms around her, fast and hard, pulling her to him and taking her mouth with his. His lips were cool and firm on hers, the taste of whiskey mingled between them. When he urged her lips open, a novel sensation captured her nerve endings, sending pleasure sweeping through her. Pleasure which intensified as his kisses turned hot and demanding.

He took the next button on her gown between his thumb and forefinger and pushed it through letting out a low moan when he tore his mouth from hers, kissing her cheek, her jawline to her throat. She shivered as his mustache and lips touched her bare skin above the opening of her dress. Her hands fisted in his jacket, his scent of saddle soap and fresh starch from his white linen shirt filled her senses. While she became delighted, confused, and yearned all at the same time, he seemed to be driven by a more purposeful force.

He crushed her mouth against his again. His tongue slashed and probed for hers, she opened, welcoming his skillful exploration. A desire she had hoped to inflame in him she never expected to turn into a hungry desperate need from her as well. Never having experienced anything like this, slow, then fast, gentle, then rough. Fingers caressed her ears, slid down her neck and arms, then to her waist, over her buttocks. His hard length pressed her against the white oak barrel. Hot heat blossomed throughout her body. In no hurry, his right hand inched up and around and captured her breast. Seconds passed before she pulled away. Catching her breath, she tried to read his face in the fading sunset filtering between the whiskey barrels, but he had stepped aside. Had he expected her to slap him? She couldn't, wouldn't. She turned and fled.

****

Just as well. He watched her black flounces disappear in the evening twilight and stood there a minute before patting his pockets. Damn, he wished he had a cigarillo. But he'd quit the habit a year ago when Doc told him his sense of smell could be affected by nicotine. A disaster for any distiller.

He spied past the rows of barrels, wondering if she had been an apparition. He had heard she was a looker. But nothing prepared him for the moment the golden-haired beauty first descended the staircase at her home. He admired her poise and courage as she faced for the most part male visitors, watched her vivid green eyes scan the room as if assessing each mourner. Why, she had even stared him down. Pen ran his hand over his thick hair, shaking his head.

All the women in her family were beautiful, even that battle-ax aunt of hers. Her mother was still handsome, despite personal suffering and a recognizable addiction to Mrs. Winslow's Soothing Syrup or whatever quack drops doused with morphine she imbibed.

He shook his head again. Should have known better than to rush his fences with Chloe Tanner. It'd have been wiser to treat her like her family's Number Five, take her down slow, savor the amber nectar, and wait, wait for the pleasure kick you knew would come.

A familiar shuffling made Pen turn.

"Thought you two might want some coffee." Milo advanced carrying a wooden tray holding a pair of hot steaming mugs.

"She's gone back to the house."

"Well, here." He handed off a coffee cup to Pen and took the other for himself. After taking a swallow, Milo nodded upward at the old man's office. "The stable boy brung a message. Those Yankee press varmints hitched a ride to the train station with the city slicker lawyers. Looks like you got the carriage house to yourself tonight. Want to walk over to the stable? Heard you got you a nice new piece of horseflesh. Like to see for myself."

"Sure, let's go." He handed over the mug. "I left my saddlebag there when I rode in. Need to pick it up."

Chapter Two

Three hours later, Pen weaved his way up the carriage house stairs into the converted bachelor quarters. The dwelling had been part of the Tanners' first homeplace, but Tom Tanner ordered plans, razed the old house, and built a modern new Victorian mansion on the original foundation for his growing family. The annex stood detached from the new residence, and Noah had taken it over for his own once the new home was completed.

Pen pushed the heavy door open and staggered in, dropping his bag in a chair by a table. Someone had lit a small wood fire in the fireplace. When he stepped toward it, a slender figure rose from the wing-back chair facing the fire.

"It's about time you got here," Chloe Tanner exclaimed.

Stunned, Pen looked around the room for anyone else. It appeared she was by herself and dressed in a modest white night robe with, it would seem, a white nightgown underneath.

"How'd you get in here?"

She tilted her head toward a closet door. "There's an entrance through there—a kind of secret passageway."

"Where's it go?"

"Back to the cellar in our house."

"Well, you need to head right back the same way you came." He placed his hat on the table and took off his jacket and hung it on the back of a chair, but not before retrieving a pewter hipflask.

She smiled and walked over to where he stood. "I want you to make love to me."

Pen unscrewed his flask, deciding to humor her.

"Sorry, I don't make it a habit of bedding innocent young maidens, no matter how much I enjoy kissing them on personal tours of their property."

"I'm experienced."

"Are you a whore?"

"No." She flinched her head back.

He raised his flask to his lips never taking his eyes off her and took a long swig. "Excuse me, I don't mean to be inhospitable," he said, holding out the whiskey to her.

Shaking her head, she stepped closer and took her hand and ran it up and down his shirt sleeve. God, she smelled wonderful. And he had not missed how nice her robe clung to her curves as she strolled toward him. Her eyes sparkled from the reflection of the oil lamp on the table, like deep seawater he should steer away from.

After spending time in the barn chewing the fat with the stable hands and passing around moonshine—on a distiller's property no less—her scent of roses and oranges sent shudders of pleasure flooding through him. A sudden ache to touch, to explore, to sweep the figure in front of him into his arms intensified. He pulled himself away to gather his sanity. Stepping back, he glanced around, sizing up the situation.

Most likely she was pregnant. Must be a married man she'd met back east, someone who couldn't marry her. But damnation, if forced to wed her after compromising her tonight, he'd wind up controlling the biggest distillery in the state. Not a bad tradeoff for accepting someone's by-blows as his own. He glanced at the door he had walked in minutes before. There was a solid lock on it.

Hell, he didn't want to end up like her father. Have some jealous man bust in while in flagrant fornication and shoot him in the back because he was with that man's woman. That was the first and last hanging he'd been to in his life. It took less than sixty days for the law to try, convict, and hang the man who killed Chloe's father.

"Should have shot him in the arse," his pa said as they hastened away from the hanging. "Can't no account shoot a man in the back no matter what he done."

Chloe walked over to the bed and removed her robe, placing it on the chair. After pulling away the covers and crawling into bed, she laid her head on the pillow. Like burning rays from the sun, her long golden locks spread over the pillowcase.

"I think I'll lock this door," he said sidling to the entry. *Damn, not going to risk any chance of being added to the "Tanner family saga."* He turned once again, taking in the scene before him, curious to how far she'd take her little performance. "And better go ahead and take off your gown, you won't need it either." My God, was this what moonshine on top of fine whiskey turned him into? *I'm the one acting like some cynical, shameless third-rate matinee bit player. Can't believe I'm talking like this. But if she's seducing me...?*

She sat up and drew her nightgown over her head and tossed the flimsy piece aside. Never taking her eyes off him, she remained sitting in the bed. All the air compressed out of his lungs. If he had ever seen a body this beautiful, it wasn't in this life. No comparisons to any real woman he knew or from books, paintings, or statues. Her breasts were as full as he imagined, firm creamy skin, with the lightest pink tips that puckered in the cool of the room. He pulled his stare from them to travel down to her flat stomach, if pregnant, she showed no signs.

Well. I'm no angel, he repeated to himself as he began unbuttoning his shirt. *The last time I checked, red blood runs through my veins. And right now, it's pulsing through me like water through a firehose.*

The aftereffects of too much drinking might have clouded his brain but not the automatic response surging through him as he stared at her. His ability to scramble out of his clothes was also not impaired, not with the naked vision before him. She sat watching his inelegant stripping, her green orbs growing larger and larger, taking in every inch of his physique.

He had never thought of his trim frame and toned muscles being uncommon among men, but her appreciative gaze was almost enough to make him blush. When he dropped his drawers, she stared at him like she had never laid eyes on an aroused male before. Had her experience always occurred under the cover of darkness? And what of her experience?

He plunged into bed, desiring only of pulling her gorgeous form to his hard one. He wrapped his arms around her, holding her soft supple body against him. Any restraint gone to hell, he ran his hands up and down her back and buttocks, smoothing his hands over baby soft skin, clasping her tighter, convincing his muddled brain she was real.

Taking less time, he kissed her. Sweet cool, insistent kisses, which, with every pass, became more and more intense. Intuition told him she mimicked his actions, each claim of her mouth, every stroke down her back, she repeated, returning each embrace with enthusiasm. He wanted to go faster, was very near frightened by how badly he desired her, but a heightened awareness singed through his mental fuzziness of the rare nuance of what he was experiencing.

Releasing her, he propped himself up on his elbows and searched her face in the pale gleam of the oil lamp. Her heavy-lidded eyes opened and focused, settling on him. He combed his fingers through the thick waves of her amber hair, swirling an errant lock around a knuckle. With his thumbpads, he leisurely traced the outline of her darkened brows, curling below her jawline, back to her unadorned ears.

He curved his hand between them caressing her breast, her delicious fullness filling his hand. He lowered his head and kissed one breast, taking her nipple into his mouth. At first, she stiffened, then her arms encircled his head keeping him to her bosom. Lifting his head to the dip of her neck, he took deep, savoring breaths of the sweet smell of her.

He pressed his lips back to her face, her mouth tender and pliant as if begging for more gentle caresses. With a muffled exclamation, he kissed her again, taking her tongue into his mouth to share the remnants of the lingering whiskey flavor, then inhaling the taste of her again. No need to hurry. No one would pull her from his arms. Let the experience evolve. Let her open to him.

Seeking her core, he moved his knee between her legs to press them apart, to welcome him to her, to allow him to pleasure her. Her breathing was heavy, pulsing. She smelled of innocence, of promise, but no question this was seduction. There was only one reason good girls defied society's mores—to claim a wedding ring. He nuzzled her neck as his hand stroked the outer folds of her sex. She quivered with each play of his hand. His agonizingly hard body pressed in closer. His fingertips delved into her silkiness before slipping a finger inside her. She writhed back and forth and sought his lips for more kisses, trembling as she pushed her pelvis against his hand.

In his fogged brain, he thought whoever the son of a bitch who had been before him had to have been a poor lover. She was experiencing something different. Maybe it was a stableboy, some fumbling in a hayloft, a forgettable experience. Some predatory rake, a banker or lawyer, or God forbid a preacher who plied her with seductive ploys.

He longed to make love to her in the real sense of the word. Leave her with a memory, one she would keep, smile about in secret, treasure. "My sweet," he whispered in her ear.

"Ohh," she moaned. "Please, Pen."

It was too much. He could not delay, could not wait for one more second to make her his own. He wanted to go slow, but his mind went senseless with her shivers and squirming, the grasping of his shoulders so tight her nails scraped his flesh. He thrust inside her.

She jerked back.

He was afraid to move. My God, she was a virgin. *Was.*

"Chloe?" He opened his eyes, nudging her, so she would look at him. Trusting dark-green eyes stared back at him. "I'm going to, I have to, I need to," he gasped as he held himself above her.

"Don't stop," she whispered.

He didn't.

****

He lowered his head, kissing her long and hard, and gently moved inside her once again. His sure thrusts swept aside any last twinge of pain. She clung to him, a tight coil of passion bursting within her. The sounds she made foreign to her essence, she twisted beneath him, her hands winding through his hair, panting sweet breaths in his ear.

Oh, the foolish books, the frivolous novels, the fantastical stories overheard from servant girls while hiding under stairs—none remotely prepared her or came near to describing what was happening to her at this moment. This strange, breathtaking thing, his taking of her, this welcomed invasion of her body by his, now sending a myriad of sensations tumbling through her. She ached to cry with happiness, pleasure, exhilaration, never imagining the intensity of emotions they shared. A desperate sob rose in her throat. Sweet bliss. Gentle, loving kisses soothed her trembling.

As the shattered pieces of her world fell to earth, Pen found his own release as he plunged once more within her. His shuddering weight collapsed on top of her. For a brief moment everything stopped. He rolled onto his side and pulled her to him, curling her back to his front, fitting them like spoons. He kissed her ear, then her cheek, muttering unbelievable words of love all the while holding her tight to him. Gradually, their breathing returned to normal in the comfort of matching heartbeats, not sure which one drifted off to sleep first.

She woke to a log falling, sputtering sparks onto the hearth, then felt the nudging of a hard body behind her. A muscled arm twisted over her, and a hand massaged at her breasts. It was Pen's. Still on her side, she reached her right arm around to feel the powerful length of thighs and the hard impediment throbbing against her. Her fingers found his manhood, curled around him. He turned her to him and kissed the 'O' her mouth was forming.

All measured and gentle lovemaking swept away. This time their joining was unrestrained and deliberate. Scorching pleasure under the blazing heat of two bodies, searching, discovering, and ending in a synchronic finale. This, whatever it was, the coexistence of their pairing, was a hard realization. One without the other, could not take place.

****

Never before could he remember having slept so sound after a night of lovemaking that the sun rose and blazed to its full morning strength before he'd even opened his eyes. Pen lifted his head, then dropped it back to his pillow. This was what raw moonshine did to any fool stupid enough to taste more than a swig or to outdrink the other men who sampled the spirits Homer Burns sent as a bereavement offering. Moaning, he clutched his head as he swung his legs to the edge of the bed. He rolled his neck, unequivocal memories from the previous night pierced his brain. A quick struggle to bound into his clothes was delayed by what he saw when he passed the empty bed. One female under fifty resided in the entire household. And that was Chloe Tanner. He did not want to lead credence to speculation to whoever did the laundry in this home. He jerked off the sheets and threw them in the bathtub across the hall pouring the last contents of his whiskey and cold water all over them.

By the time he exited the annex, the Tanners' touring chaise was drawn in front of the residents' entrance. The family's steward supervised luggage being loaded in the rear trunk. Chloe stood off to the right of the vehicle dressed in a traveling suit. He walked up to her raising his hat.

"Good morning," he said slipping his arm through hers and pulling her down the gravel walkway away from the coach. "Are you going somewhere?"

"Yes, I'm leaving for Boston, then on to New York."

Pen released her arm, raised his hat again, and ran his left hand through his dark hair. He opened his mouth to speak, then shook his head. "Last night?"

"Yes?"

"We need to talk about it."

"Why?"

"Why the hell not?"

Her face flushed, and she sought to look away from him. But he wasn't having any of it. He gripped her upper arm. "Another habit I don't make is jumping in and out of bed with women without so much as a by your leave. And I know you had never been with a man in your life until with me last night."

"I know. And I will be forever grateful for it as

long as I live."

"Are you crazy? Because you are talking crazy?"

"No."

"So, what the hell are you talking about?"

"I'm getting married, Pen."

He froze.

"I'm marrying Peter Tanner."

"The old tycoon in New York?"

"Yes, he's a fifth cousin of mine. It's all been arranged." She paused momentarily. "You were at the reading of the will, Pen. We have no cash reserves. And when both my grandfather and brother died in the shipwreck, we lost... The stock has plunged to almost nothing."

"Borrow the money."

She laughed.

"Sell it to me."

"You couldn't raise that much money even if you mortgaged everything you owned."

"You don't have to do this."

"Yes, I do. There are so many people who are counting on me. Depending on me."

"Believe you me, I know too well about a family's ability to pressure young women," he sneered.

"It's not solely family depending on me, but my employees and others throughout the county, this state, and America. We have distributors everywhere, including overseas. Don't pretend you wouldn't do anything yourself to save your business—be truthful."

"And us? What happened? Did last night mean anything?" His brows furrowed. "Why? If this was your plan?"

"I wanted to know what it was like to lie in the

arms of a young man. A man to love me with passion and sweet words—just one night. Do you remember some of those words? I do. I always will." Tears welled in her eyes. "I knew I'd be leaving Tennessee and wouldn't ever have anyone like you to love me. I didn't want to wish I'd not taken the chance. I don't regret it. I hope you won't either."

"You can't…"

"Why not? You men do it all the time. My own father…" She pressed her lips together in exasperation.

"No. I'm not like other men. Not like your father," he said. "And what of the chance you might become pregnant?"

She jerked back drawing a deep breath. She gripped her fingers around his forearm and dragged him farther down the path.

"I'll not let any man claim my child as his own," he said not lowering his voice.

She bit her lip. "If that were to be the case, I'd send you a telegram."

"And let the whole county know before me?" he exclaimed rolling his eyes.

"A cryptic message."

"A cryptic message—my God what kind of cracked-brain people raised you?"

She stopped and seemed to be working out an explanation all over again. "You would do the same, Pen. You would do anything yourself. If you had an ounce of heart, you wouldn't betray me."

"I'll run you down—I'll sue you. I'll do whatever I have to if I find you are having my child."

"You'd do that?'

"Yes."

She knotted her hand to her forehead. "Surely there's little chance you have to worry. I promise you I will send word. Please, please let me go. I must."

She looked up at him. Tears swam in those beautiful eyes, and he knew she had won.

Her chin lifted higher, and she pulled her shoulders back. "I must go now." Turning, she walked back to the carriage where the driver stood in the offing to help her in. Her mother had already been assisted in and waiting.

****

Chloe took her seat across from her mother, refusing to look her way. Instead, she stared out the window as the coach drove down the lane.

"What did Pen Kittrell want?" Regina asked.

"Me."

Her mother glanced at the figure in front of her house. "Honestly. The nerve of that man."

The nerve. Yes, but it was her nerve. It took every drop of strength in her body not to collapse in Pen's arms. She knew, once she spoke the truth about saving the company and contending he'd do the same if he were in her position, he'd let her go.

She peered out the carriage window. He watched the coach travel the short gravel drive. The last image she glimpsed was him removing his hat, slapping it against his thigh, tugging it back on his head, and walking away.

Chapter Three

Washington DC, March 1893

"Damn shame to have to have our country's inauguration a full four months after the election. It is 1893, for Pete's sake. Shouldn't take as long to count and tabulate votes as elections did almost a century ago," Winthrop Owens, the Tanners' lead attorney, grumbled. He and his wife accompanied Chloe and her mother from the Richmond Arms Hotel to the inauguration ball.

She had visited the Smithsonian in Washington DC once before, after it had opened as a museum. But on this cool March night, the gothic red-brick monstrosity designated as the official site for a ball celebrating President Cleveland's second inauguration had been transformed. Not that she would have minded at all the location of any ball she was attending for her first public event after her family's funerals. If required, she would have gone to a party in a pig stye. Tomorrow, she would be traveling back to Oak Hollow after a five month's absence, no expectation of fancy balls in that tiny town.

Her heart skipped like a young girl as she was handed down from the Owens' carriage. Music from a whole orchestra streamed from the museum's expansive exhibit area. Gas lights, red, white, and blue bunting, silver streamers, and gold fringe burst from every nook and cranny of filigreed woodwork like fireworks exploding from within.

Excited, she peered at the crowd on the dance floor and smoothed her hands down her gray satin gown. From the second the couture house presented the sketch of her first dress out of mourning in New York, she looked forward to this moment. The design was a work of art. A satin silk creation enriched with beads embroidered in an iris pattern graced a flowing skirt. Short puff sleeves and a low-cut square décolleté. The pointed midriff made her waistline appear infinitesimal. She opened her fan of hand-sewn figures appliqued on black lace tulle. Tossing her head, she smiled, knowing the many mirrors would catch her single hair ornament, a large diamond barrette placed among the looped tresses.

She walked dutifully behind her mother who still insisted on wearing all black six months after her son had passed. Mr. Owens deposited the ladies along the dance floor and left them in pursuit of stronger drink and conversation with the chief justice whom he had just spied. The orchestra's opening reel was followed by a repertoire of waltzes. Chloe tapped her satin slippers to the music, enjoying the colorful mosaic of satins and silks glittering around the ballroom. As she gazed at the swaying dancers, she caught a black and white figure wending his way through the purples, pinks, and blues toward them. *Oh, too late. He's already seen us*, she muttered to herself even as she attempted to hide behind Mrs. Owens' stout form.

"Mrs. Tanner, Miss Tanner," Pen Kittrell said with a noticeable emphasis on the *Miss* when he approached them. He bowed over Mrs. Owens' hand, who appeared to relish the attention of such a handsome gentleman.

"I haven't had the pleasure," he said as Regina made the introduction of their attorney's wife. He flashed his white smile in both matrons' directions, then asked if he could take Chloe out on the dance floor.

"Oh, no, Pen. We are still in black gloves," her mother protested.

"Regina, my goodness, let the young people dance," Mrs. Owens said as she tapped her fan against Pen's arm, intimating for him to take his partner off and to leave any arguments to her.

"You're surprised to see me," he said as he guided her to the dance floor. "Did you suppose your distillery would be the sole contributor to the President's re-election campaign? Enough to garner invitation to his inauguration ball?"

She pressed her lips together, not answering as she placed her hand upon his shoulder to begin the waltz. *Why, oh why, does he have to look so handsome?* When he stood before her mother and Mrs. Owens in his formal wear, she felt her body heat rise and could not help her stomach from fluttering. His stark white shirt and tie contrasted against his tan skin and dark hair. And impossible to avoid noticing how other young women and even matrons turned their way when he circled her waist and piloted her to join the other dancers. No wonder any woman not needing spectacles would note how fine-looking a man he was.

"No, I shouldn't have been surprised." Her guilty heart thumped as he navigated her with expert steps around the other couples.

"I tell you what is surprising me," he said. "The

fact I'm not addressing two Mrs. Tanners. I presumed I'd be offering you felicitations the next time I met you."

"Don't act like you don't read papers. You know my company recovered significant remuneration from the accident which killed my grandfather and brother."

"Yes, I did follow. I was astounded. I congratulate you on the attorney team you employed. Treble damages for a maritime accident. Impressive. Honestly, what I would have predicted, if anyone had asked me, was—there would be no wedding. Didn't pull that off, did you?"

"Well, you don't have to look so smug."

"I feel smug. All these gentlemen are staring at you, wondering what you look like without your clothes on," he said as he twirled her around the ballroom, "and I'm the only one in the room who does."

She missed a step and had to rely on him to catch her when he uttered his last statement. He tightened his arm about her waist and whisked her with proficiency toward the outer edge of the dancers.

A heated flush raced up her neck. How she wished she could dance and use her fan at the same time. "You are so rude and cruel to bring the past up."

"Say again? I distinctly remember you saying you would never forget."

She bit her tongue and breathed in, expanding her display of bosom from her already regretful choice of décolleté.

"May I compliment you on your appearance tonight. You look quite beautiful. In fact, I imagine I could almost encircle my hands around your entire tiny waist. Which speaking of being cruel—I have yet to receive any telegram from you."

"There was no need—as I am certain I assured you—it was only one time." She regretted the words as soon as they were out of her mouth.

"It was two times, if memory serves me right."

She reached out to grab his shoulders as she faltered multiple steps. Their bodies pressed close as Pen whirled her about cradling her in his arms to keep her from tripping. He wove her away until they were almost at an alcove.

Acutely aware of her breasts pushed against his warm body, she mustered the strength to pull away. She lifted her head, staring up at him. "I can't go on talking to you, much less dancing with you, if you are going to behave this way toward me."

"That's all right. I was just leaving for something a little less tame when I caught sight of you." His eyes were deep and dark, his voice unsteady as he stared back at her.

"Thank heavens," she said as they stopped in the enclosed terrace. She jerked away and snapped her fan open. Filigreed beads flew, hitting Pen's evening jacket before rattling to the floor.

"But I have two other important things I want to tell you tonight. However, I'm afraid the subject matter would precipitate you much distress and cause you to do more than blush once you hear them. You're at the Richmond Arms, are you not?"

She fanned her burning cheeks, refusing to answer.

"I'll be at your door at two a.m. Let me in."

"You're insane."

"Not any more than you. Both you and your mother are registered in the Presidential suite. Regina will be sound asleep once she takes her nightly dose of elixir. She'll never hear the door open."

"You're out of your mind. I'll not do it."

"Well, your mother might not wake up, but everyone else on the hall will once I start pounding on your door. Two o'clock. Expect me." He bowed and left her standing in the alcove all alone.

****

The soft chimes from the hotel mantel clock rang twice. Chloe opened her suite door a crack to peek out to the hallway. Not sure what she should anticipate. She glanced in the direction of the elevators, no one there. Thank goodness. But before closing the door, she spotted Pen coming up the staircase. He sauntered down the hall toward her, still in his formal wear, twirling his top hat, whistling a tune, as if he hadn't a care in the world.

Of all the... If she weren't so mad. When he reached her door, he bent at the waist giving her a mock bow. She grabbed his arm pulling him inside, not allowing him a chance to look about the salon. With a death grip, she pulled him through the open door to her bedroom. As she turned to close the door, he placed his hat on the nearby table and started removing his jacket.

"It's hot in here," he said loosening his cravat, taking a long perusal of her gauzy night robe. "How high do they have the radiators turned on in this place?"

"You can't stay," she said, handing him his jacket before retightening her robe's sash. "Tell me what you wanted to tell me, then you must go."

He withdrew a sterling hipflask from his coat pocket and held it up to her. "You might want to take a sip of this before I begin."

Alarmed, she plopped down on one of the table's cushioned chairs. "What is it? Has something happened back home?"

"Yes." He passed the flask in her direction before placing his jacket on the back of the other chair. "I'll cut to the chase. Do you know there is a boxcar full of unlicensed Tom Tanner's Number Five headed to a New Orleans port tomorrow from the Oak Hollow train depot?"

"We never ship on Sundays." She exhaled in relief, smiling at his poor joke. "You're misinformed. Why would anyone try to pass on such a bald-faced lie? Who's behind this?" she asked scrutinizing his face. "Besides, you know nothing goes out from the rail yard unlicensed. The state of Tennessee established the licensing station for both our distilleries the previous decade. Why are you spewing this vile rumor to me?"

"Sorry, not a rumor." He took out his pocket watch. "In fact, I have an observer who witnessed the loading of the whiskey crates a mere eight hours ago. Took half a day to do it by his account."

"A whole boxcar?" She completed a quick calculation in her head. "That's one thousand crates of whiskey, close to half a million dollars. Couldn't happen. Nothing gets past Milo."

"Milo hasn't been around. His nephew came and collected him and took him home to Pine Bluff last week, something about a stomach ailment. I suspect he was poisoned."

"This is too outrageous. My foreman sick? Me not knowing? Why are you making this up? Is this some kind of retaliation against me?"

" 'Fraid not, sweetheart."

She reached across the table and took a healthy swig from his flask. Ignoring the first commandment of whiskey drinking, sip, don't shoot. The whiskey, strong but very smooth, was like a soft fire traveling down her throat. "Don't believe you."

"Call the train station master."

"I'll telephone Jed Sanders, my general manager."

"Who do you think is behind this?"

She stared in shock at Pen. Her body tensed. A rage simmered under her skin, absorbing what she heard was in all probability true. How dare he, that low down scoundrel of a manager. The minute her back was turned. Without thinking, she brought the flask up to her mouth and took another pull. Pen stretched his arm over and grasped the container.

"No. He wouldn't," she insisted, shaking her head. After a long stare at Pen's impassive face, she said under her breath, "I never did trust the man."

"How well did you know him?"

"Not well. Noah liked him. Said he was a wizard with numbers. Freed my brother to manage our overseas accounts and allowed Grandpa more time to supervise the tastings."

"What about when you visited during summers?"

"Well, last summer I stayed at Oak Hollow two weeks, then Noah and I went to New Orleans to visit our distributors. Funny you should ask. He told me then he did not like the attention Sanders was paying to our mother." She let her hands slide to her lap, sniffing as she recalled the past. A tightness in her chest returned.

"Here's your options, my dear. Call the station master in the morning, stop the train, and fire Sanders in the process. Or. Or you can marry me, and I'll do it for you."

"Marry you?" She laughed incredulously. "Be serious." She cocked her head to the side and narrowed her eyes, wanting to perceive his suggestion. "If this is true, I can take care of the matter myself. I'll put in a telephone call to Rob Terry at the station first thing in the morning and get to the bottom of this whole sordid tale. He'd dare not make a move without me giving him the final okay."

"Good girl. Hold those civil servant's feet to the fire. Might telephone the sheriff too while you're at it," he said as he took a drink.

"Thank you, if this is true, for bringing this to my attention. I don't want you to think I'm ungrateful. I guess I've been gone too long. I'm leaving to go back tomorrow." Chloe frowned as she remembered there was something else to ask. "You said there were two things you had to tell me tonight, what was the second?"

"Did I?"

"You know you did."

"Yes. I wanted to tell you I wanted to kiss you. Couldn't tell you that on the dance floor either." Her left hand lay across the table. He rubbed his hand over hers, gradually slipping up the flowing sleeve of her night robe. She wrenched away, but not before grabbing his flask and taking another sip.

"Are you not afraid of reaching a stage of inebriation I might be tempted to take advantage of?" he asked cocking one dark brow up.

"No. As you have reminded me several times earlier tonight—there is not anything else you could do with me you have not already done."

"What a little innocent you are, Chloe." He circled the table and took the flask and pulled her up from the chair. "I've thought a lot about you these past few months. Didn't want to. But did." He wrapped his arms around her and nuzzled her neck.

She breathed in the butterscotch whiskey and sandalwood smell she associated with him. Wanting to see if there was truth in his eyes, she pushed against his chest, locking her arms to study his face. Could she believe him?

"Tell me you want to kiss me too," he whispered.

Inch by inch she moved in, surrendering equal distance. Finally, their lips met as if no time had passed between them—a continuation of their night together a few months before. She could taste the heavy sweetness of the whiskey they had drunk, smell its heady scent, but it was his mouth, his touch that made her dizzy with desire. One greedy kiss followed another. Her pulse thrummed, luxuriating in the feel of him, the hard-muscled physique she remembered so well. She knew a fierce yearning, a need to touch. She slid her arms between them to undo his shirt button as his hands sought to unknot her robe.

"Why do you have so many clothes on?" she asked exasperated, contemplating even more buttons on his embroidered vest.

Letting out a low laugh, he hooked his arm around her tighter, pressing his lips against hers before deepening the kiss. "Is this the whiskey talking?" he asked in a hoarse voice.

"Does it matter?"

"No."

In one swoop, he gathered her in his arms and

carried her to the bedside. He yanked off the thick coverlet before turning to reclaim her. Between fervent kisses, they managed to undress him, for her it was one untying of a sheer silk bow, and her virginal white nightgown, part of an anticipated trousseau, dropped to the floor.

She tipped her head back, whispering his name as he lifted her onto the bed and arranged her so she laid beneath him. Marveling at how perfectly his body fitted to hers, his strong calloused hands caressed, fondled, and stroked her full length. Her flesh tickled and tingled; emotions teemed with anticipation. Bending his head, he kissed her breasts, suckling before blowing cool puffs of whiskey breaths over her taut nipples. Pen burnished her skin with liquid swirls from his mouth. Reveling in the claims of his kisses, the possessive strength of his embraces, and the assault on her consciousness, she surrendered to his torment.

Pleasure flooded her entire being as she shivered with desire. Was she dreaming? She had replayed in her mind multiple times the night they spent together in Tennessee. Was Pen truly making love to her again? She ached for him. Craved for his slow, deep drawl to whisper words of love in her ear once again. Wished for those roguish eyes to spark and glow with desire for her. She yearned for him with her whole body, heart to heart, skin to skin, not leaving an inch of space between them.

His lips traveled from her breasts, bestowing kisses to her belly, circling warm kisses from her navel journeying further to plunder her body. He glanced at her. A devilish grin filled his face. He scooted down and lowered his head between her limbs pushing her legs apart with strong arms.

"Merciful heavens," she gasped, shutting her eyes tight. Frantic, she curled her fingers in his thick hair. Never pausing, he soothed her anxious movements as his lips glided over her, swirling his tongue across and in places arousing senses she didn't know existed. All of it sending her spiraling down a breathtaking path, making her jerk and squirm and quiver and rock.

Never had she read, heard of, or imagined this kind of experience. Never in her friend's father's library, or in the medical manuals they filched from the hospital pharmacy had she ever encountered a description of such surreal magnificent torture. Where would you learn these things? In brothels, from courtesans? From concubines? Or harems? That was it. She was captured and being ravished by some dark sheik in the middle of the Sahara Desert. She was sweltering hot. Her mind spun. Her capturer was relentless in his assault, of what he was doing to her, cradling her in velvety carpets, now throwing her up, up to the top of the tent, then bouncing her back to him. Up, down, in the air, weightless in the sky, then falling down to be captured all over again.

"Oh, oh, oh...." She surely died. Her body shuddered one final time. With effort she opened her eyes, trying to focus. Gold lights flashed, no, twin turquoise jewels stared at her.

"Chloe, Chloe—you're beautiful," he whispered. He rose to cover her body with his and kissed her like she was a China figurine that might break.

"Pen." She wrapped her arms around him giving him assurance she was not about to shatter.

He took her then, in the traditional sense. Slow

measured thrusts, that soon turned relentless, then ended in quick explosive jerks with Pen muffling his moans into her pillow. Sighing she shook her head in wondering disbelief before kissing the top of his. This—whatever it was, could not happen with anyone else. They were one. The feelings, the chemistry of which she knew about—the blending, the melding, the merger—once you found it—of two souls—was like the cultivation of fine whiskey. And just as satisfying.

****

Chloe reached across her bed and felt for the warmth which had cradled her most of the night. Gone. She lifted her hand to the pillow next to her head and touched a flower laid on top. She opened her eyes. It was his boutonniere he had worn to the ball last night. A door creaked and someone trod across the thick hotel carpet and threw open the room's curtains. The sun's first rays pierced the room. Chloe clutched the white rose to her bare breast as she scooted beneath the covers.

"Milady, do you want me to bring you some hot cocoa or would you prefer your bath first?" Brigette Flanders, her new lady's maid, asked as she gathered from the floor Chloe's nightgown, then bathrobe.

"Hand me my robe. I'll take a bath first. They keep these hotel rooms so warm. I was burning up last night," she said as an excuse for lying naked in her bed. Her maid passed her the garment without exhibiting any skepticism on her face. Bridgette had been employed for her by her aunt right before Chloe had returned to Boston for the trial after Noah's funeral. The young woman with bright red hair, sparkling blue eyes, and a mass of freckles had just immigrated from Ireland. She was a quick learner and interested in pleasing her new employer, and, best of all, she was close to her age, a welcome diversion from being surrounded by her mother, aunt, and their clutch of matron friends. The two young women enjoyed each other's company as they traveled from Boston to New York, then at last down to Washington to attend the presidential inaugural.

"Yes, it's hot as blazes in here, as my mum would have said."

****

Pen walked into the hotel's elegant dining room and stood scanning the early risers seated for breakfast.

"A table for one sir?" the host asked.

"I'm going to wait for my party. Will you send coffee to the reading room?" Pen turned, detouring past the frosted glass partitioned area where they kept a bank of telephones for guests to use. No one was inside. As he turned, a heavy hand clamped him on his shoulder.

"Hey there, Kittrell, you're out early."

"Benson Graham." Pen turned and greeted one of his school classmates from New York City who moved back after graduating to join his family's law firm. A very successful and lucrative practice, one which benefitted from the many lobbying efforts generated from keeping close proximity to the capital. The two men stepped out of the way as a bellboy passed them carrying a vase of two dozen pink roses to the elevator.

"Bet I know who those are for," Graham said. "Saw who you were taking for a spin on the dance floor last night. Too expensive for my blood. Still, love to dream about those arms holding me close. Don't get your hopes up, old chum. Not like in school where your handsome face and charming smile stole every girl we fancied away from us on the dance floor. Gossip around the tea tables is the rich ole tyke up in New York was just biding his time."

"What are you saying?"

"Word was the jury would be more generous if they perceived the victim as a destitute young thing without a penny or a man to turn to. Money follows money, doesn't it my friend? Or is it money marries money? My mother said it will be a September wedding. Makes sense, after a year of mourning and time for everyone to return from the Hamptons for the summer. She said plans were for Chloe to marry in the same church as her parents did."

Pen's gut tightened like a steer being roped for branding. "Wish I could stay and catch up, but I'm expecting a telephone call, if you'll excuse me."

Graham would know, he gritted his teeth. There wasn't much he'd miss in the way of rumors involving financial transactions flowing in every direction up and down the East coast. So had that been the plan all along?

Was Peter Tanner going to start with marrying the heir to Tom Tanner Whiskey, then one by one take possession of each and every one of them with his unscrupulous business practices? Like falling dominos, all the monopolistic trusts—railroads, oil, sugar, tobacco—was whiskey next? Of course it was, he wasn't that big of a fool.

So, what was he in this calculation—before being blindsided by a takeover of his own company by another robber baron? Was he one more sweet memory for her before having to spend her wedding night with a groom old enough to be her grandfather?

****

Three hours later, he spotted Chloe pacing back and forth on the train platform for westbound departures. When she recognized him, she raced up to him.

"Pen, I had a nightmare you got in a carriage wreck or something. A relief you're finally here. You'll be so proud of me," she bubbled grasping his arm. "I've already telegrammed the Oak Hollow station master, and I telephoned my local attorney as well. They've assured me they will deal with everything until I arrive home this afternoon. Hurry." She pulled at his arm again. "I'll tell you the rest onboard. The train is leaving in minutes."

"I'm not going back to Tennessee today."

"What?"

"I have other business in Washington I have to take care of."

"But I thought...last night? You...?" she asked in bewilderment.

"Last night was beautiful. I will always remember it."

She remained motionless. Her mouth open. Speechless.

"I've come to say goodbye." He raised his hat. "You've saved your company, Chloe—now comes the hard part. Let's see if you can run it."

He nodded, replaced his hat, turned, and walked away.

Chapter Four

Chloe stood, rooted to the spot at his revelation. He surely didn't mean it. Did he? Her eyes widened. She shook her head in disbelief. He threw her words from months ago in her face. A mirror image of the last time the two of them said goodbye. Except today, the roles were reversed.

She clutched her hands together, willing him to turn and come back. A hansom cab waited, he opened the door and disappeared inside without so much as glancing her way. Just as he had stood a few months ago and watched her walk away.

Did last night mean anything? Isn't that what he asked her before she strode away from him on her front lawn. Cold invaded her body, she raised her fist to her mouth biting her thumb hard. Her heart seemed to stop. Shock, disbelief, hurt—she shrank back from the emotions hurtling at her, stumbling against a concrete planter. Late passengers pushed by her, jostling her as they rushed to catch the train. The station master shouted out his last "All aboard" call. Unable to move, she remained frozen in place.

"Miss Tanner, I've been searching everywhere for you," her maid professed, out of breath as she approached her. A locomotive whistle blew, causing Chloe to jump. Bridgette touched her on her arm. "Are you all right?" She peered down the platform, one man could be seen driving away in a cab. "Did that man say something to you?"

"Yes, no, it doesn't matter. Let's go. Is Mother on board?" Chloe asked, then cleared her throat to cover the tremor in her voice. She allowed her maid to drag her numb body onto the railroad car and settle her in their compartment. An ache, a throbbing pain at the base of her neck, traveled up to her temples. Had Pen abandoned her on the train platform? Had that really just transpired? She took off her gloves and rubbed the sides of her face.

"I'm going to go get you a glass of water," her maid said.

"Bridgette, walk with me to the dining car. I need some coffee. Chloe, do you want to come too?" her mother asked as she stood.

"No, you both go on. I'm fine."

Oh, Lord. The aftereffect of staying wide awake most of the night, then working the entire morning to rectify her problems back home, at last caught up to her. Her cheeks heated as she recounted last night. Making love, heart-stopping, earth-shattering love through the wee hours of the night. She knocked her head against the train's window. How in the world could two people do those things together and it not mean anything?

He said he was different from other men. But was he the same after all? Anger simmered. Oh, the humiliation. Of all the heartless, vindictive, and merciless acts he had perpetrated on her. To have made such mind-bending love, then walk away. *Just like I did to him*. Had she bruised his ego so bad? They say men weren't as vengeful as women. Bah! Well, the score was even now. And she would never have to see him again. But that would be impossible living in the same town. *Well, I'll refuse to recognize him.*

He had mentioned marriage. When she laughed in his face, was that when he decided to seduce her this time? To give her something to remember him by? Or had it been his plan to win her heart, then gain her distillery? Well, marriage to her meant one thing. Control.

If you can run it. That's what he had said to her. *He's insufferable.* What a low down—she didn't know the worst word to call him. What did he think she had been doing back East for the past four months while her lawyers prepared for trial? Every single minute she could spare was spent consulting with managers, accountants, and professors all sharing business plans, explaining balance sheets and stock shares until she was ready to jump in front of a train at the end of the day. A condensed lesson—yes—yet a solid foundation on how to run her company. *Well, we'll see who can best run a whiskey business.* He'd thrown down the gauntlet. This was war.

"Here's your water, Miss Tanner." Bridgette had opened their door and held out the glass. Chloe sat motionless staring up at her maid's comely face.

"Thank you, Bridgette, thank you very much," she said as she accepted the drink. Chloe gave her a genuine smile for the first time in the long morning. *Yes.* She glanced back at her maid, *I'm quite certain I can get a least one McCoy away from Pen to accept my opening for a new general manager. Those Irish McCoy triplets who'd trained and worked under Kittrell would fall over themselves trying to curry favor from such a delightful colleen.*

"Where's my mother? Chloe asked.

"Back in the dining car. She met someone she knows. Said she'd return in a few minutes."

"Help me gather a bunch of handkerchiefs. I have some unpleasant news I have to give her."

"Will we need smelling salts?"

"No, she won't faint. More likely she'll be searching for some of her elixir."

When Regina returned to their compartment, Chloe endeavored as best she could to tell her mother what had transpired at Tom Tanner Whiskey in their absence, and what she prepared to do to rectify the situation.

Her mother's shock, denials, then defense of their general manager's activities were so stringent she failed, thankfully, to ask Chloe how such sensitive information had come to her notice.

"Mother, I'm going to have to take care of this as soon as we arrive home. Do you understand?"

Her mother nodded at last. Huge tears ran down her still youthful face. She cried until they approached Knoxville. With three more hours of travel time, Chloe allowed Bridgette to help locate her mother's tonic so she could get some rest.

While her mother napped, Chloe steeled herself for the confrontation she knew would be coming. *I'll see Mother safely home, then summon Sanders to my office at the distillery, but not before I secure two of my biggest plant workers to accompany me. Oh, how I wish I had Milo with me.*

****

Oak Hollow, Tennessee
Chloe watched passing rail signs indicating they

would soon reach her childhood home. Her head had long since cleared, but her mouth continued to stay dry. She swallowed again, then rubbed her arms, trying her best to get her blood moving after staying stationary for so long.

A whistle blew as the locomotive pulled to a stop at the Oak Hollow station. The depot and terminal were one of the four-thousand residents' proudest achievements. The townspeople were aware they could not hold a candle to the larger cities in the state, having neither the monies nor political pull. But through community fundraisers and local craftsmen's ingenuity, they built a majestic Victorian train station. One, though on a smaller scale, rivaling any other Louisville and Nashville station along the L&N lines.

Chloe stepped out with her mother and Bridgette on the wide veranda with its beautiful filigree iron banisters and columns. They walked through the mahogany paneled doors to the huge general waiting room with its intricate tile work floors and imported stained glass windows.

"Regina, Chloe, welcome home. So glad you made it back safe and sound. I hope your trip was restful and relaxing." Jed Sanders' loud pompous voice boomed as he stood in the center of the terminal like a general presiding over troop inspection at a military parade. He was a tall man, with a receding hairline of blond hair which failed to cover a balding head. His ruddy complexion, thick neck, and piercing eyes always reminded Chloe of a weaving cobra ready to strike.

"I'll have your trunks unloaded without delay and we will be on our way to Tanner House." He motioned to someone before stepping forward to try and take her mother's arm.

Chloe scanned the room. She recognized her attorney, Wendell Deane, standing by the Station Master's doorway. His Ichabod Crane physique misled many an opposing lawyer. Rob Terry exited his office to join him. Milo, nor her head groom, Jenks, were to be seen. She stole a glance in the direction Sanders had motioned earlier and glimpsed a pair of brawny men barring the exit doors from the terminal. A family with three young children and a couple of businessmen were waiting by the ticket counter. Two elderly ladies and a maid carrying a baby walked from the restrooms.

After Sanders signaled him, a bifocaled rail agent approached her with a clipboard and extended a pen. "Miss Tanner, if you'll just sign this bill of lading, we can assist you with your leave-taking."

She had been a witness to a similar scene like this once before. Her aunt had been defrauded out of investment funds from her long-standing bank in Boston when they changed ownership. A private meeting had been requested by her aunt to rectify unauthorized transfers after repeated requests to reimburse her failed to take place.

She had accompanied her aunt that day and prepared to wait outside the manager's office while her aunt finished conducting her business. Instead, when the two entered the bank, the new manager pretended to befriend her aunt in the lobby. He began making a grandiose speech on how she misunderstood the risk of her investment, wishing in retrospect she had taken the advice of a man. He was daring her to cause a scene in the busy lobby in front of customers, some of them their neighbors. She recognized the same condescending smile and patronizing platitudes in her distillery's general manager. An evident attempt to thwart her intentions, misdirect and subjugate her authority.

"Bridgette, take Mother into the women's waiting room. Mr. Terry, may we use your office, and join us as well. Mr. Deane, Mr. Sanders, please, let's go in."

"Presently, however, Miss Chloe, we need your signature, so we do not delay the outgoing train. The rail workers need fifteen minutes to attach the rail car," Sanders said. The clerk stood by his side and held up the clipboard once more.

"I have no rail car going out today," she said as she swept into the station master's office. Her manager stamped behind her. *Concentrate. When you turn around, pick a spot between his eyebrows to stare at.*

"You need to sign this document immediately."

"Excuse me?" She wished she had all five feet nine inches of her aunt's height, but she drew up straight and raised her chin squinting at a wrinkle on Sanders' forehead.

"Don't be highhanded about this, Chloe. As general manager, business transactions you may not be cognizant of take place twenty-four hours a day." His face became redder and redder as his frustration increased. "Transactions which make you a great deal of money, I may add."

"And you, Mr. Sanders? It has come to my attention that one thousand crates of unlicensed Tom Tanner Tennessee Whiskey have been loaded on a railcar which you have been attempting to ship out since this morning."

"I'll not listen to any more claptrap. You need to

sign this document now."

"Or what, Mr. Sanders?" She stared at the selected spot on his forehead. "Mr. Deane, is one of those men standing outside on the platform an agent of the Tennessee government tax office?"

"Yes, ma'am."

"Please give them instructions to inspect the cargo inside the solo boxcar my manager has waiting to be attached to the departing train."

"You can't do that." Sanders fumed.

"I can, and I am."

"Miss Tanner, we have already checked the contents of the rail car. It's full of whiskey, and there's not a single licensed crate on board," said the rail worker.

"May I have the clipboard, please." The bookkeeper passed it over with shaking hands. Chloe took the clipboard, grasped the document, and handed it to Mr. Deane. "Please preserve this as evidence of what has been attempted today. And please proceed to take down any statements from witnesses who overheard the events that occurred this evening. Including this: Mr. Sanders—you are fired. You have three hours to remove any of your personal effects from Tom Tanner Whiskey's distillery and plant and from the manager's cottage we have provided you the past four years."

"No way in hell—"

"If you do not comply with this request—I will swear out a warrant for your arrest for trespassing."

"Why you little—"

"Please do not waste any more of my time." She pulled her gloves on tighter as a form of dismissal expecting the man to display fangs any moment. "Or

I'll be encouraged to file a claim of embezzlement against you on behalf of Tom Tanner Whiskey to the tune of half a million dollars."

"You will regret this, little lady," he sneered, stomping out.

Chloe took three steps back and collapsed in Mr. Terry's swivel office chair. Her heart must be beating so hard the two men who remained with her could see it pumping through her chest. When she looked up at their faces, she witnessed a gleam in Mr. Deane's eye and a knowing grin from Mr. Terry.

The station master walked behind his desk and opened a drawer. "I just happen to have an open bottle of Number Five right here in my bottom drawer. I think we have time for a tiny sip, a 'welcome back to Oak Hollow' toast, don't you agree, Miss Tanner?"

"Certainly, gentlemen."

****

"I'll be right in, I'm going over to the stables first," Chloe said as they pulled up in front of Tanner House.

"Chloe, it's so late, can't you wait until the morning?" her mother pleaded.

She was out of the carriage and down the gravel path before her mother could voice another argument. A faint light burned inside the interior of the stable. To her delight, a familiar whinny sounded as she darted in.

"Têtu, Têtu." She sprinted to the last stall. Her white mare's head protruded over her stall's door and neighed in recognition. "I've missed you, girl," she said as she rubbed her favorite horse's nose.

"Well, well, well, who have we here?" her head groom asked as he stepped from the tack room.

"Jenks, I am so glad to see you. I thought you'd be

at the train station."

"I was planning on going but thought better of it. Too many suspicious things going on here. So many, I was beginning to regret my decision to leave Boston to come work for you."

"Oh no, I need you here. And Milo too, have you met him, is he back?"

"No, but I imagine he'll be returning soon, a cantankerous character, I've heard tell. Word 'round the stables, he was poisoned." Her longtime groom brushed his salt and pepper locks and sent her a questioning look. "Not accusing anybody of anything, but I don't care for that general manager of yours, I can tell you. One of the reasons I stayed behind today."

She clasped Têtu's mane. "Do you think they were going to poison my horse?"

"No, I'd guess they aimed to steal her. Two men I never saw before came in here earlier and took off with a couple of horses. I haven't seen them since."

"Jenks, I fired Mr. Sanders today. Hopefully, he's got his personal things and by now has left—for good." She turned to look at her mare once again, laying her head next to hers. "First thing in the morning, I'll be down to ride you. I promise."

Chapter Five

Chloe rose at dawn the next morning and threw on her riding habit. As she raced by the barnyard she whispered, *I'll be there in a few minutes, Têtu. First there's something I have to do.* She entered the main door to the distillery and scurried up the stairs to the row of offices. Pausing at the open door of her fired general manager's office, she wavered a minute before entering. There hadn't been time the night before to check and see if he had cleaned out the office of his personal effects.

This morning, the desk stood almost cleared. No calendars, no memos, or messages stacked or spread about, no remnants of pending business. She leaned over the desk and pulled one of the leather notebooks from the shelf above. Turning the pages she noted the listings of the maturation year, the barrel demarcation, and location in the rick house of every whiskey barrel on site. A miracle it was left undisturbed. She reached for another volume. This one included account names, dates, and sales. Jed Sanders was indeed their numbers man—a good one—however, a dishonest one.

She pulled the center drawer ajar, nothing but a few pens, then grasped the right side drawer and opened it. A small stack of opened letters lay within. She took a step back without turning her gaze from the top one. On letterhead stationery from Kittrell Distillery was a missive from Pen Kittrell. She saw his signature at the bottom.

Footsteps scuffed outside the office. She jerked the letter out and stuffed it in her habit's skirt pocket. A grizzled face stuck his head into the doorway.

"Milo Knox! I've never been so glad to see anybody in my life," she squealed throwing herself into his arms. "I heard you were ill?"

He tut-tutted her, releasing her grasp. "It'll take more than some spoiled game to take me out. I rode in this morning. I learnt you arrived last night."

"I did. My plan was to go riding first but had to come over here and check on things. Milo, I fired Jed Sanders yesterday."

"Good riddance. Picked up the news in the barn from your head groom you brought with you from Boston."

"Milo, tell me about Pen Kittrell. I met him again when I visited DC."

He studied her, giving her a penetrating look. "You aren't thinking about selling out, are you? Come with me." He grabbed her arm and pulled her down the stairs trudging across the distillery's center walkway. He stopped at the mill room door and opened it wide. The grain, still sorted by hand then hammered to a grist, covered the floorboards of the entire room. Milo leaned down, scooped up a handful, and pressed it in her hand.

"It all starts here. With this golden grain, so unimpressive, it could be mistaken for dust. But Tanners mind you, Tanners turn this grain into magic. More valuable than gold because we make it ourselves, we create it right here. Nothing like it on Earth. Why it's loved throughout the world. You wouldn't take that away, would you?"

Tears glistened in Chloe's eyes. *He's right. This is not about me. Not about money. It's about each and every one of us and everything we've worked for. And about what we leave when we're gone.*

"You go on your ride now. It will give you lots of time to clear your head. Beautiful day for a ride," he said before tromping away.

It wasn't until she was at the stable door that she realized she was still holding the handful of dried grain in her palm, and that Milo had not said a word about Pen Kittrell.

"Jenks, Jenks," she shouted. "Have you got Têtu saddled?"

"We've been waiting on you. This girl is ready to run."

"Jenks, before I go, I have to ask a favor. Mother threatened me last night. She says I can no longer ride horseback all day around the countryside. Says it's too unseemly now that I'm the head of Tanner's. You have to find me a curricle. Order me the fanciest, most conspicuous model you can buy. Something Bostonians would think was outrageous."

****

From his vantage point in the second story of the county courthouse, Pen observed the train depot's warehouse where Kittrell's and Tanner's liquid gold was loaded. Two days a week loads were sent down the line, some to interior cities, some to seaports where their product shipped around the world. The dock was also where equipment and machinery, anything besides a passenger, unloaded. Two rail workers opened a boxcar, and another motioned for something to be removed from the cargo hold. The early spring sun reflected off bright shiny metal as soon as the object was shoved out of the freight car onto the unloading ramp and unpacked from its wooden crate. It was a liquid filling machine.

He had coveted that new piece of machinery for months. An unrivaled invention that could do the work of six men instead of one in the space of an hour. Designed to place liquid within the container at the fastest, most efficient pace ever, while breaking production rates globally. His mouth watered as he continued to observe the men unpack. He knew, without a doubt, who purchased it. Damn, putting her insurance money to good use it appeared. Or was this an engagement present from the disgustingly rich Peter Tanner? Perhaps? Who knew with her.

Maybe she had taken his challenge about running her company to heart. Word reached him at almost the same moment she confronted Sanders in the train terminal. Firing him on the spot. It took nerve. And hadn't she already poached one of his lead managers? Damn those McCoys.

So what was her plan? Was she going to run her distillery or sell out to those robber barons? She was just a little bit too cozy with those aristocratic criminal captains of industry for his comfort. *Well, I'm not taking any bets off the table yet.* He'd laid odds with himself that she'd last six weeks tops before packing up and heading back East. But that spinster aunt who raised her in Boston must have infused some backbone into her as well as Yankee ingenuity, because she was still here.

A chalk scratch on one of the tally blackboards in

the massive walnut-paneled room of the exchange hall drew his attention. The bustling area was filled with men holding their clipboards and counters. A quick calculation told him at least half would lose their jobs if Tanner Whiskey went under. It wasn't just family and plant workers who would be affected if no one took the helm at Tanner's and sailed it through tough times.

He pressed his head against the window. Below, a smart two-passenger curricle turned into town from the east side. Grinning, he watched two women try to navigate the flimsy gig over the railroad tracks. He recognized Chloe instantly. However, the other young woman was unknown to him. As they bounced across the tracks, the girl sitting beside Chloe, her hat fell off. Bright red hair glistened in the afternoon sun. Ah, that would explain McCoy's defection. Hell, if she hung around his distillery at closing one Friday, he'd lose half his crew.

He turned his attention to the woman who most disturbed him. The one who invaded his dreams and interrupted and distracted his thoughts at the most inopportune times. What a beauty. Not only attractive, but intelligent, witty, and indecipherable. Unpredictable for sure. He shut his eyes as intensifying memories of their intimate moments together closed in. His heart pounded harder and harder.

I'll be damned if I let some nineteen-year-old chit—or was she twenty now—change the way I live my life. He swore an oath. For sure, he was developing sympathy for her deceased father—probably seeking comfort with a sane woman in his bed—not some looker like his wife. What was it his Pa used to say— "you don't look at the mantel when you're poking the fire."

Impatiently, Pen pushed away from the window.

****

"No, don't pull back. Hold them loose but firm," Chloe instructed Bridgette as they crossed the second set of tracks.

One horse jumped forward as the other stopped, almost sending Chloe over the stylish curricle's front bar. Laughing out loud, she righted herself, and then replaced her broad-brimmed straw hat.

"You're doing fine," she encouraged her maid, whom she had insisted learn to drive.

She had purchased the lightweight two-wheeled vehicle when first returning to Tennessee. Smiling to herself, she recalled the memory of her request to her head groom. She had laughed until tears spilled from her eyes when, a week later, she spied the red wheels of the newly acquired curricle with its shiny black exterior and Kelly-green leather seats being driven into the stable yard.

Riding her horse and driving her curricle soon became the best way to escape routine. A regimen dictated by the duties and responsibilities of her job as owner of Tom Tanner's Whiskey, but also one imposed by herself to escape unsettling memories. At odd times, she found herself thinking of the man she had told herself she'd never think of again.

Chloe had never believed in love, at least the romantic kind. Her aunt's house held zero novels or books of poems; her friend's borrowed regency romances presented little insight into anything she could relate to. Growing up, her own parents offered no picture of affection or even devotion to each other. If she had ever harbored hopes of a happy marriage and children, they were dashed before she could reexamine them. And up until a few months ago—she had not been interested in any man—until Pen.

She ignored the fluttering in her stomach, the tingling of her skin, her heart beating fast when she recalled a smile, a laugh, a kiss. She found herself wondering during the workday what he'd be doing. Would he be tasting his whiskey? Was he checking his inventory? Would he be ogling the newest series of popular advertising lithographs, those colorful works of art featuring beautiful women to be pasted on posters, labels, and calendars?

When she first returned from Washington a mere month and a half ago, managing the distillery consumed every hour of her day. Waking every morning, she headed straight to the plant. There in her grandfather's own cramped whiskey-tasting sanctum, she oversaw the nosing and tasting alongside the other master distillers of each readied batch of whiskey. Mornings made the best time for this important activity because one's palate was fresher. Her grandfather had schooled her well. One's tastebuds dulled as the afternoon approached. Better to take a nap he would say.

She spent her afternoons with lawyers, distributors, and vendors instead. At four o'clock she dismissed them all, cleared her desk, walked out, and locked the office door behind her. Free to clear her head, free of disturbing memories. Jenks had her horse saddled and waiting, or the two would take the curricle around an improvised track behind the distillery.

She was a decent driver but sought to become better and her own practice track helped her. Most men touted a love of horses and speed, and she determined to test the theory herself once she became proficient as a driver. She had invited one of her most irritating and tedious vendors, who had given her a headache overexplaining a contract that day, for a spin in her new vehicle. She chuckled at the memory. By the second turn on the oval track, a breathless excuse was given, and the businessman couldn't be on his way fast enough.

She knew she was still being tested, particularly after firing their longtime general manager. And she already had two strikes against her, being female and so young. But so far, she'd kept her promise to work harder and longer than anyone else on her payroll.

Today, she made up her mind, would be her first day to end her self-imposed exile from the public and drive her new curricle into town. Besides wanting to supervise the offloading of her new bottling machine, every household was responsible for donating a minimum of five bushels of ramps for the May Ramp Festival. Jenks loaded on the distillery's wagon their share of ramps, the local excuse for an onion, but in actuality just a wild leek. The open baskets generated a pungent and malodorous odor on this unusually hot day in early May. Rather than ride alongside him, Chloe decided she and Bridgette would accompany the load but take the curricle and travel ahead of the wagon. With the intention of giving her maid driving instructions along the way, the two set out.

"You're doing great, but hand me the reins," she said as they crossed the railroad tracks. "We're in town now, and the horses might become edgy."

Once they turned onto Main Street, Chloe wished

she had insisted on a different transportation mode. She had no desire to draw extra attention to herself today. Well, too late now. She motioned for Jenks when she spotted her cousin Maggie about to enter the bank.

"Bridgette, you go on with Jenks to take the ramps. I'm going to visit with my cousin. I'll wait for you here, then we'll go for some ice cream."

She waved to Maggie before pulling the vehicle to the curb. As she climbed down, she stopped. A beautiful gray mare was tied right at the hitching post. The horse appeared unattended. Chloe dug into her dress pocket and pulled out the last of the tangerine she had sucked on during the hour-long ride.

"Do you like tangerines?" she asked. "My mare does." She patted her mane and fed her the pieces one by one. "What a gorgeous horse. Do you know who she belongs to?"

Before Maggie answered, heavy footsteps coming down the wooden sidewalk abruptly stopped.

"If you keep petting her like that, I might become jealous of my own horse."

Chloe jumped back like she'd been stung by a red hornet. Appraising her in a cavalier manner, from under the shade of the covered walkway, was Pen Kittrell. She figured she would run into him at some point. In truth, he was the primary reason she had avoided coming to town. Seeing him standing there with his unfashionably long hair brushed away from his chiseled cheekbones and well-defined square jawline, with his full mustache topping lips which…

Until this moment—she felt safe and confident enough, sure she could handle their meeting without awkwardness. He gave her a playful smile, one which conveyed mischief along with amusement. Pictures flashed in rapid succession, like the moving photographs at the zoopraxiscope at the Massachusetts State fair. Images of him, her, and the things they had done together. She ignored the jittering feeling in her stomach, and the sudden warm flush traveling through her body. *Mercy*. Well, time to face the music.

"Oh, sorry, just admiring her. What's her name?" she asked, wiping her hands on her dress. She twisted an escaped tendril of hair with her thumb and forefinger, annoyed with herself for being bothered by his self-assurance. And for foisting such vivid sensual memories on her, she shook her head. She rapidly regretted not sending her foreman to supervise the transporting of her new bottling equipment rather than come to town herself.

"Patience."

Seriously. Onlookers gathered about admiring Chloe's curricle. As folks circled around inspecting her gig, she patted Pen's horse again.

"Fine looking piece of horseflesh," Jenks said as he and Bridgette walked up and joined Maggie and Pen. "I'd like to take her out for a gallop."

Agreed guffaws sounded. Pen stepped off the sidewalk and started to unwind his horse's reins from the post.

"You know," Maggie announced, "Chloe has a mare."

"And I'd say she'd measure up to your sassy gray anytime," Jenks bragged.

Pen smiled, then glanced over at her. "Does she race?"

Someone else on the sidewalk whistled.

"Of course she can. Fast too," Chloe answered without thinking through the implications.

"Care to arrange a little wager?" he asked. "Not skittish, is she? About showing what she's got?"

Chloe's cheeks became hotter and hotter. Would he ever stop with his rude insinuations?

Maggie's groom came in from who knows where and suggested, "What say we have a race between your two mares? We could have it at the end of the ramp festival. Ain't nobody using the track then. Let's do it then. Gives us two whole weeks to get ready."

"Tanner's versus Kittrell's. Battle of the Stills," someone shouted out.

"Great publicity," Pen added. "What say you?" He mocked a pleading look her way.

"Well…" She started calculating the positive press an event like the one suggested might generate. News articles about her distillery, ones that conveyed the solvency of her company after such a turbulent year, could be just the thing. Before she said yes, hands were shaken, times decided, and the decision regarding jockeys seemed the sole item left to be discussed.

"I know you think you ride fillies like none other, but you can't ride her yourself, that wouldn't be fair. We have to have neutral jockeys." Chloe couldn't believe she was even entering the discussion.

"Agreed," Pen said laughing in agreement at what she said.

"What about the prize?" another voice in the crowd asked.

Chloe was past worrying about her burning cheeks, her whole body desperately hot. She wanted to duck and run, retreat somewhere from this suffering discussion.

"I know what I want," Pen said, reading her up and down. Chloe swallowed, her chin dipping. "An afternoon picnic provided by and accompanied by Miss Tanner if I should win. And you Miss Tanner, what would you like?"

She took in his self-satisfied expression and without a pause said, "Your hat."

There was a collective "Whoa!"

"And for you to shave your mustache."

More moans from the men. "Doesn't seem quite equal," a male voice proffered.

"I think it's more than equal," Pen said with a grin that indicated some secret knowledge while rubbing his smooth black mustache.

"Let's shake."

Chloe lifted her hand. She knew she was bested. At least for the moment.

"I've promised my maid ice cream. We must be going."

"I haven't had the pleasure." Pen stepped forward to meet her lady's maid.

"Bridgette Flanders, meet Pen Kittrell."

The young woman dropped a curtsy, blushing profusely under Pen's engaging smile. "Good day, Mr. Kittrell."

"Maggie, join us for ice cream?" she asked her cousin, in effect dismissing Pen. As she watched him mount his horse and ride off, she had to ask a burning question.

"Why has Pen never married or at least become betrothed to some girl? Most men in the county are married and have two kids with another on the way by the time they are his age. In fact, my own brother and Pen both have to have been anomalies." They walked on down the sidewalk with Bridgette following.

"I'm flabbergasted. Don't tell me you've never heard the story about Pen and Noah fighting over the same girl?" her cousin asked as they continued on toward the drugstore. "My pa said he wouldn't have been surprised if we had the first duel in the county since Andy Jackson's nephew rode over and shot one of the Sawyers."

"No, I've never even overheard a whisper. Who was going to tell me—not my aunt. What happened?"

"Well, they say Pen was courting heavy a new girl who moved south with her relatives. They bought a tract of land on his side of Wishbone Falls. When summer came, and he and Noah swapped places at the distilleries—Noah met the girl himself. Daisy. That was her name. Daisy Pemberton. Got to remember that. Anyway, when Pen got word Noah was stepping out with her—Pen got so furious he almost busted up his family's still fighting Noah over her."

"What happened?"

"Just what everyone said would happen."

"Which was?" Chloe blurted out. Impatient for her cousin to finish.

"Like I said, she was a Pemberton. One of those families who relocated from up north to start the temperance town of Harriman by the Emory River. Well, her granddaddy wasn't having his only granddaughter marry the heir to a whiskey distiller—which could mean either Noah or Pen."

"And?"

"Came over here with Great-Grandma Pemberton

and took her away. We never heard hide nor tail about her again."

"Noah or Pen didn't try and get her back?"

"Nah—Noah started keeping company with some gal down in Bald Gap, and Pen—well, he started going to Nashville a lot. And you know what kind of women Nashville is full of."

Chapter Six

Chloe's lungs expanded to their fullest. Intense satisfaction surged through her as she walked through her distillery. A place that awakened all her senses. She remembered coming here as a child, thinking it was paradise. No longer an idyllic playground, it was her business now, one she intended to preserve. She smiled as her workers went about their duties, felt the warmth from the open fire that heated her pot still, and listened to the hum of the mash turns.

Since returning from the east, she had carved out a schedule working with each stage of the whiskey making process. She peered into one of the giant wooden fermentation tanks, watching it bubble as the yeast converted the sugars in the mash to alcohol. She thanked her lucky stars they were blessed with plentiful pure water. Tennessee's limestone geology, which removed the iron from water, was essential to distilling whiskey. Confident her family's secret recipe mix of corn, rye, and malted barley and their unique strain of yeast separated Tom Tanner's Tennessee Whiskey from all other competitors, she took measures like her grandfather to carefully guard samples.

She stepped down from the tank platform and walked to the base of the pot still, following the path of its swan neck. Vapor traveled up, which was converted into liquid when it reached the top. Later, she'd take a fresh look at the design of their pot still. A detail they would have already dealt with if they had relocated the distillery a few years ago to Willow Ridge. She glanced at the clock hanging on the far wall, reached behind her to untie her apron covering her riding habit.

"I thought you'd be over supervising the installment of your new liquid filling machine?" Milo asked, stumping up to her clapping his hands.

"Is everything all right?" She stopped working the apron strings' knot, staring with unblinking eyes at Milo. She had witnessed him clap his hands thousands of times after pouring distillate on them, giving them a vigorous rub, and then smelling the new whiskey on them. He did this to see if he could detect the nose of their yeast with corn being their dominant grain. Why was she so anxious today watching him perform this automatic regimen? Her heart pounded at the thought of something going wrong with her whiskey.

"Yes, everything's fine. Was watching my nephew separate the heads then the tails from this morning's run. Just making sure it was done right. And it was," he said with obvious pride in his voice.

Chloe breathed a sigh of relief. All distillers knew the amount of heads and tails allowed to bleed into the heart—the finished product—was one of the ways a distiller determined the distillery's house character. Some made this decision based on time and proof. Others, like Milo, preferred to taste and smell for cuts. Either way, it was an art, one that could take years to master.

Failure to properly cut, then test the run could result in severe sickness, blindness, or even death if imbibed. The heads and tails—the front and back of the distilling process—both contained indigestible compounds. She recalled the year a drifter broke into the distillery and tried to steal the liquid before it was sent to the beer tank to begin the main run. His mistake, and one that could have cost him his life—thinking the liquid was what was sent to the spirit safe before making its way to the barrels.

"I was watching the machine installation earlier this morning, I'll leave it with you. Everything looks to be running smoothly. I'm heading to the stables. I'm meeting Pen Kittrell so he can see the horse he's racing against this weekend."

"Well, he's not at the stables. He's over at your bottling machine watching how it works."

She tried not to show her surprise before hastening down to the distillery's bottling section. Pen stood in a line with some of her other employees marveling at the new machine's capability. A certain amount of fine alcohol had been lost in the initial hook-up. But like everyone present, watched in amazement as the new machine took on a life of its own as a dozen bottles of whiskey filled within minutes.

He waved when he saw her and ambled over to join her.

"I saw a prototype at the industrial fair in Chicago last year, but this one works circles around it."

"I'm pleased you are taking such an interest in my distillery; nonetheless, I believe I was expecting to meet you at my stables."

"Are you ready?" he asked ignoring her insinuation.

"Certainly. My groom is waiting on us."

****

"Têtu, an unusual name for a horse. It has a meaning?" Pen asked as she first mounted up at the stable.

"Yes, it is French for stubborn."

"Well, Stubborn meet Patience," he said, introducing the two horses. Her mare snickered, enjoying the way he rubbed her head between her ears. "Which way?" he asked after mounting his mare.

"Let's head north," she called, giving a backward glance to her groom riding behind them. Pen leaned over his horse's mane to pat the gray mare's neck. He sat astride at ease on his mount, forcing an earlier fleeting thought. No person could be all bad to have such a magnificent horse like Patience.

"I didn't know you rode so well," Pen complimented Chloe after a few minutes of riding. They reached the pasture on the east side of the watershed which flowed down the Wishbone. She had agreed to meet him to introduce him to her beautiful mare after he protested the unfairness of not having met his competition before Saturday's upcoming race.

"I recall you told me you broke your arm in a fall from a horse," he said when they trotted along a well-worn bridle path. "Sometimes an accident like that keeps people from getting back on a mount. Congrats to you for not letting the fall impact you."

"My riding lessons were one of the few ways I could escape my aunt's smothering supervision. I wasn't about to give them up."

Gazing at her with a certain focus, he said, "You know, I honestly don't know a lot about you."

Really? Just more about me than anyone on this earth. Hoping her hat shaded her burning cheeks she turned in his direction. "What do you want to know?"

"Well, what's your favorite color?"

"Blue."

"Favorite flower?"

"I should say rose, because they smell so wonderful, but they are too hard to grow and have thorns, so I'd say hydrangeas. I like history, of course, since I lived so long in Boston, and I can play poker."

"Play poker? One talent I wouldn't have matched you with. Didn't have a professional card shark hired by your aunt to teach you which cards to hold did you?"

"No." She laughed. "Noah and Grandpa taught me."

He turned and studied her face. "Bet you're a good card player. Ready to give these girls a run?"

"Wait, what about you?"

"Blue's my favorite too, but roses for me. Thorns and all." He gave Patience a swift kick to her flanks and set off to the top of the pasture.

"Wait," she called. *Just like a man*. Avoiding any questions about themselves. Compressing her lips, she nudged her mare and chased after Pen. He took a hard left, abandoning the plowed acres, and guided the horses over land yet to be felled, covered with hardwood trees and thick pines. The undeveloped property followed the steep rocky shoreline of the fast-moving stream. A narrow path Pen selected forced them to trot single file, offering no opportunity to talk even if they could hear each other above the splashing water below.

She rode behind, staring at his strong back and shoulders for another quarter of a mile. How odd to talk and ride together as if nothing had ever happened between the two of them. Had he put aside the memory of the times they made love, slept side by side, albeit even for a short while, and never thought on it? Merciful heavens, she had. Thank God, his back was turned to her. She uncoiled her hands around the bridal she had twisted up. Hurt as she had been when he abandoned her in DC, a persistent inclination made her believe his actions were in response to how she had first abandoned him. She had not yet reconciled her heart to where her true feelings regarding Penland Kittrell stood. *Well, I can play his game too. I'll not give you the satisfaction of knowing what my feelings are either.*

At the crest, Pen turned his horse into a clearing. The Wishbone tributary plummeted into two separate channels, thereby giving it its name. The Kittrells had settled to the west side, while the Tanners chose the east. Chloe pulled her horse alongside Pen's and gazed at the panorama before them. Her heart rate ratcheted up as she marveled at the scene. Admiring the unspoiled nature before her, she sat transfixed, aware the view had changed little since the time Indian tribes roamed its shores and paddled down the narrow streams. A lone eagle swooped down the river, scanning the clear waters for prey.

"I've been here before, but I approached from a different direction. A wagon trail comes in from the other side." She pointed to an opening a few yards away between a rock crevice.

"This is our legacy, Chloe. Got to take care of it."

He turned and took the path she had mentioned, then stopped a short distance later to study something at the water's edge.

"Have any of your people been up here lately?"

"No, why?"

He lifted his arm motioning Chloe's groom over. "Know anything about this?"

"No. Beavers sure didn't do it. Man-made. Fairly well-fashioned," Jenks answered.

"Just what I thought." Pen dismounted and inspected the collection of chopped tree trunks, tree limbs, and grapevines attached together forming a crossing from the east side of the Wishbone. "Not any point constructing a bridge here with two ferries about a mile upstream." He glanced again up and down the waterway. "Come on, let's head back. I need to turn for home as soon as you and Jenks reach the north pasture."

"Is something wrong?" Chloe asked.

"Nah. Just a little strange."

When they reached the well-trodden path lane leading toward her homeplace, Pen did not dismount. "I'll see you Saturday."

"Yes, Saturday. Be ready for a hot shave," she teased.

"I was just going to say I like fried chicken and cherry pie." He tipped his hat to her and then was gone.

****

Chloe stood by the window in her plant's office looking out. She turned when footsteps stopped outside her door. Corbin McCoy knocked on the open door's glass pane.

Hiring him to replace Jed Sanders as general manager turned out to be one of the best decisions she had made since taking the helm at Tanner's. His efficient, constructive, no-nonsense manner made him invaluable to her within days. Clearing his throat, he asked, "Miss Tanner, may I ask a favor of you?"

"Why certainly," she answered in a surprised tone.

He raised his eyes to smile back at her, encouraged, his stocky frame stepped into her well-organized office. Not for the first time, she wondered how his mother produced three such full-sized males at the same time. "The thing is—I've asked Miss Bridgette to the dance this Saturday night at the end of the Ramp Festival."

"Wonderful."

" 'Cept she won't go—on account, she don't know how to square dance. I've told her it ain't no big mystery. You just follow the others and listen to the caller." He flushed touching his forehead.

"Go on." She noticed his long-suffering smile. "How can I help?"

"I thought if you would be in agreement, we could have a little practice session tomorrow, then Miss Bridgette would be more willing to accept my invitation."

"You've given this some thought," she said while rearranging some papers on her desk.

"Yes, I can clear some rugs from the parlor of the manager's cottage leased to me, and there's a piano inside."

"You found someone to play?"

"Yes, ma'am. I've got everything ready; I just need you to come too."

"Me?"

He brought his gaze upward from the floorboards and looked straight at her. "Well, we need four square dancers for her to believe it's going to work."

"I see." She brushed her hands together. "Tell me when I am to show up for this critical dance lesson."

"Tomorrow, five o'clock," he responded with an appreciative nod. "After whistle blows for the last shift."

****

"Good afternoon."

Startled, she turned. Pen Kittrell's deep voice greeted her at her manager's cottage front door. He was dressed in top-boots and leather breeches, a soft cotton shirt with a narrow, dotted tie, and suede jacket. And looking way too delicious.

"Mr. Kittrell." She smoothed the skirt of her forest green dress, hiding her surprise and wishing she had worn a nicer one.

"I'm here to help out one of the McCoy triplets, not sure which one, but my step-mother insisted I ride over to help."

"You rode Patience over?"

"No," he said with an unmistakable gleam in his eye. "Got to keep her fresh for the race in two days."

"Bart, what are you doing here?" Her short statured groom, who had agreed to be her jockey for Têtu in the upcoming race, joined them on the porch.

He doffed his hat, then withdrew a harmonica from his coat pocket. "I'm to be the signal-caller for this here dance lesson," he said puffing out his chest. "Told me to be here at five, on the dot."

As the three entered the house, Chloe received another surprise. Her head groom was seated at the piano working through the keys. "Jenks, you play the piano?"

He turned and smiled surreptitiously. The huge straight-back piano had been repositioned under the arched entrance leading into the dining room. The carpets in the hall and parlor had been rolled up and removed along with a good deal of the furniture. Bridgette and Corbin walked in behind them forcing her and Pen into the center of the room.

"Well, let's get started," Bart said.

Bridgette blushed and Corbin turned scarlet-faced as he caught Pen's amused chuckle.

Chloe propped her hands on her hips, pushing aside her irritation at this turn of events. "How do you want to proceed?" She wasn't sure how helpful she'd be, although she had learned square dances at her school and had seen them performed at festivals a few times.

"I'm going to recite the most common moves. You'll take your partner and practice them as I walk you through. Jenks is going to play, while I call. Nothing to it, Miss Bridgette," Bart reassured her. "We'll go slow. Ready? Gentlemen bow, ladies curtsy."

After his bow, Pen took Chloe's hands. "And you, Miss Tanner, are you attending the dance at the finale of the Ramp Festival?"

"No. I'll be welcoming my horse back home from a brilliant race. One I'm sure she will win."

"You're very confident, Miss Tanner. I like that in a woman."

"Circle left," Bart called. "Now allemande left. This means everyone faces their corner, take a left forearm with your corner, and circle around until you are facing your partner again."

She stood staring at Pen still holding his hands.

"Drop arms," Bart chided. " 'Do si do'—means face your partner, step past each other passing right shoulders and without turning around, step back, then step back up, passing left shoulders until you're back in place. Right and left grand."

Chloe glared at Pen as they passed their shoulders.

"Everyone, face your partner, and taking right hands, walk past each other, then alternate hands with the people who come to you until you meet your partner again."

"Am I doing it right, Bart?" Bridgette asked as she skipped through the moves.

"Yes, good job, Miss Bridgette. They'll be sets of eight dancers, instead of two sets here, so you need to keep up. But you'll do fine. Let's do a Promenade. Couples get in a skating position, men on the ladies' left side. Come on now, I know Miss Chloe cannot be the only one to take a partner ice skating. Take hands and walk together counterclockwise. Music please."

All four dancers promenaded, laughed, circled, and twirled, as Bart made the calls, then circled back to their respective partners. Seeing Bridgette's glowing face significantly lightened Chloe's mood along with the appreciation of everyone's efforts on her maid's behalf. *When I return to the house, I'll pull out my periwinkle dress to give to Bridgette, it will go so lovely with her hair and eyes.*

Jenks banged together melodies that sounded more like burlesque show ballads than typical square dance refrains. Although she had never darkened the door of a burlesque show, she eyed Pen, quite confident in his knowledge of the kind of music played at them.

She followed the tune and hummed, closing her eyes, the melody so much more fun than the dainty dances she was used to attending. Pen stepped lightly, swaying her to the song, tightening his arm about her waist. She opened her eyes and caught him looking at her in a way that made her heart race in time to the fast strains of the music.

"You dance very well, Mr. Kittrell," she said while promenading. "I remember waltzing with you in Washington."

"There's lots I remember doing with you in Washington."

Her face, without a doubt, was as crimson red as the color painted on the walls of the cottage. Too late now, she brought that comment on herself. Thank goodness he had no clue of how often she replayed in her dreams their night together in DC.

"Now Swing. Circle clockwise, let's do four turns. Then the man twirls his lady under his arm to finish the swing." Bart blew into his harmonica to warm up. "Weave the ring, just like the left-right grand you just did. Roll away to a half sashay. Ladies in, men sashay."

He's enjoying this. His movements were confident and his hands relaxed. Her heart skipped, as Pen lowered his voice to whisper in her ear as he twirled her under his arm. "I am happy to sashay with you anytime."

"Pass through, separate, and then go home. Pass on your right, turn your back, and walk around the other couples."

Jenks twinkled through the keys playing another animated tune. Bart walked over to help Bridgette and Corbin.

"You're an excellent dancer yourself, Miss Chloe," Pen said still holding her arms in a starting dance position.

"Save your pretty prose for your pony, Mr. Kittrell," she said smiling at him.

"Did your aunt also provide you with dancing instructors when you lived with her?"

"No. I learned in school."

"Ah, the school you were going to tell me about one day. What else did you learn at your school besides dancing, Miss Tanner?" he asked in a patronizing manner. "While I was being trained in the art of warfare at my school."

She wrinkled her nose. "Well, we did our part too, in preparation for war. Our whole class was encouraged to take part in nursing training. Of which, to be honest, I was not interested in. But they had a pharmacy at the hospital where we trained. So, I asked if I could assist the pharmacist. I thought working with the different chemicals in medicine would be like working here in Oak Hollow at my distillery. That it might help me. It didn't last long, the men working there were, well they stared."

"I'm sure you were a major distraction." he conjectured as they continued to promenade around the room.

"Perhaps so. Anyway, the pharmacy doctor moved me far back in the storeroom—my job—folding bandages into boxes. I was near the breakroom, it had a sink and a little beaker stove, and it didn't take long before I built a miniature still," she bragged.

"A what?"

"Let's start at the beginning," Bart interrupted. "Jenks, some music please. Gentlemen bow, ladies curtsy."

"It was quite simple," she continued.

"Circle left. Allemande left, now do si do."

"You didn't?"

"I did." She beamed. "I even shared a batch with my roommates when I snuck some back in my lunch pail."

"You surely didn't get away with this?"

"No. I think someone must have reported me to my aunt. I was altogether removed from the program. No one ever said a thing."

"These same girls you offered home-brew to, you didn't teach them how to play poker too?"

A grin escaped her. She felt sure if her grandpa were there, he'd say her dimples were showing.

"Let's try it again," Jenks said from the piano. "With a little less talking," he admonished.

Her skin tingled at Pen's touch when he took her hands again. She glanced down at his fingers interlocking hers. Long fingers, she looked up at his face, those eyes, those lips. Did he care how much he had awakened her flesh, flesh that had never known a man's touch before? She realized with distress, it didn't matter. *Nothing could ever come of the two us, better to just forget what happened.* If he'll allow it. Better to move on. She released his hands.

"Bart, Jenks, thank you both so much. Bridgette, you are doing beautifully. Stay if you want to practice some more, but I must return to the house, my mother is expecting me for dinner." She nodded to everyone except Pen, turned, and left.

"I need to be heading home too, folks," Pen said and walked out behind her.

Not wanting to appear any more rude than she felt, she faced him with a smile. "Thank you, Pen for coming. It was very thoughtful of you."

"My pleasure."

Ohh, the man was insufferable. She scurried off.

****

Damn. He stood and watched her run back to Tanner House. Shaking his head, he tried to sort her out. Impossible. She raced horses, drove a mean curricle, played poker, built a miniature still, and fired the meanest SOB manager he knew. And seduced him like...*My God*, what kind of woman was he tangling with?

****

"Miss Chloe, wake up."

"Humm." Chloe rubbed her eyes sitting up in bed. Her room was in total darkness, but she still made out the figure who was shaking her shoulder. "Bridgette, what are you doing here? What's wrong?"

"Please come. I'll explain everything. Hurry," her maid begged as she handed over her robe while Chloe searched for her slippers.

The two women slipped down the back stairs with Bridgette leading the way through to the kitchen. She pushed open the door and stepped outside with Chloe following. There, standing on the walk to the washhouse and other outer buildings, stood Pen Kittrell.

The moon was full on his face, his eyes glinted as he gave her an appraising look. She tightened the sash about her thin wrapper and combed her fingers through her tangled loose hair before eyeing him accusingly.

"What are you doing here?"

"Please, Miss Chloe, we need your help," Bridgette whispered. "It's Corbin. He's been hurt." She pulled Chloe the short distance behind the washhouse.

There she recognized Pen's light gray mare with an unconscious man thrown across the saddle. Chloe starred, incredulous, her mouth wide open. "How hurt is he?"

"Gonna live. Got in a fight," Pen said. "He was conscious enough to tell me which room was Bridgette's so I could wake her to help me get him to his cottage."

"I don't think anyone heard us," Bridgette said. "Cook stirred when Mr. Kittrell knocked on our door in the help's quarters, but she went straight back to sleep. Corbin keeps saying his key is under the home. We have no idea where to look."

"He means under the gnome. It's one my parents brought back from their honeymoon in Europe," Chloe told them, as the three led Pen's horse to the manager's cottage. "What I can't understand is why you're here helping, Pen. He's got two brothers."

"Right. Both who work for me. One of whom is my general manager," Pen answered. "Don't care to have them going over to the Red Bruin and beating the shit out of who did this to their brother, then have them both arrested and locked up for attempted murder."

"The Red Bruin?" The tavern perched on the edge of Stinking Creek. Locals called it the 'Red Ruin.' Young and a handful of older men frequented the establishment to drink cheap liquor, ogle floozy barmaids, and gamble on cock fights behind the old ramshackle saloon. She retrieved the key from underneath the yard ornament, unlocked the door, and found a lantern to light as soon as she entered. Pen lifted Corbin off his horse, carried him over his shoulder to the bedroom and laid him down. As Chloe held up the light for Pen to unbutton his shirt, she shrank back at the swollen and bloody face of her manager.

"He's just banged up, gonna be sore, but other than that, he'll be all right. No knives in this fight, just fists. Bridgette, you want to help get him cleaned up? Chloe, can you find us some water?"

The three worked frantically the next few minutes to care for their patient. After Chloe tore sheets apart, Pen fashioned some sort of brace around Corbin's midsection with Bridgette's help. When finished, Pen pulled off Corbin's boots and stood at the end of his bed assessing their handiwork.

"I believe he'll be recovering soon enough," he said as they watched Bridgette flutter about Corbin. He turned to look at Chloe. "Any way can I get some fresh water for my horse?"

"I can't believe you had Patience carry him here," she said.

"Not much choice. He'd have fallen off his own horse, that's why I threw him across mine. Come outside with me for a minute."

She passed through the doorway, then returned to the bedroom. Pen stopped her by gathering her in his arms and half-carrying her down the hall. "Let her be alone with him for a while."

"But I need to tell her he must not come to work tomorrow. Or even think about attending the race." She squirmed in his grasp trying to go back.

"I'll tell her. Come with me." He led her through the front doorway, not releasing his hold on her. Once outside he loosened his grip. "Don't you want to know what this fight he got in was about?" he asked.

Heat flushed through her body. It was impossible not to feel his muscles strain against her through the thin fabric of her wrapper. She pounded one fist against his chest.

He held her away inches from him. "Do you?" He asked again.

"All right tell me," She spit out, provoked by his behavior.

"It was over you."

"Over me?"

"Yes. It seems someone opined a very crude and disparaging remark about working for a woman boss, and he took issue with it."

Shock replaced her anger, then pure torment. Her throat constricted. She shut her eyes. The fact her name was bandied about within the debauchery of a saloon and then to have it be defended by her employee stunned her. "I don't know what to say. I would never expect and..." She swallowed hard pushing herself away from him. "I feel awful. And you, I owe you a world of thanks. I don't know how I can thank you for getting him here safely."

He took her in his grasp again, dragging her around the corner of the small house. "I think I can think of a way."

She gripped his hands between their two bodies, aware her proximity to him aroused an intense sensation. He freed his hands and wrapped them around her, pulling her in tight. He ran his hands up and down her back, down to the curve of her hip and up again.

"A kiss," was his suggestion. Not waiting for an answer, he leaned his head in and pressed his lips against hers.

Chloe trembled at the pressure of his tongue seeking hers. She tasted alcohol on his lips. How long had he been at the Red Bruin before the ruckus occurred with her manager? Inexplicably, she responded, pressing her mouth to his. Hadn't she dreamed of this moment? A shiver of pleasure centered in the depth of her body as he continued to kiss her. His hold became more possessive, as strong hands moved over the length of her.

"Come back here tonight," he whispered with a ragged breath as his hands fumbled with her sash. "Take Bridgette to her room then come back down."

Chloe pulled away and stood staring back at Pen. If she stayed with him one more minute, he'd take her completely, right there between the boxwoods. And she'd let him. She opened her mouth to speak but nothing came out. Seconds passed before she found her voice. "I can't."

Gathering her robe together, she hurried to the front door of the cottage. Bridgette stood waiting on the entrance's stoop.

"Pen is going to stay with him for a while after watering his horse. Let's go back." She grabbed Bridgette's arm and flew up the path to the main house.

****

Chloe pressed her finger to her lips when she met Bridgette in the hall the next morning. She pulled her maid's arm and slipped from the house dragging her along. "How's Corbin?" she whispered. "Have you seen him yet?"

"Yes, I went before sun-up. Sore. And so awful sorry for putting you to so much trouble."

"Please tell him not to worry. Whatever he needs, Bridgette, if you can't find it, call me." She descended the steps of the back porch, leaving without breakfast or coffee, and walked the long path to the factory. Intent on getting work done before she attended the first tasting of the day, she sent a longing glance at the stables as she passed. She would love to check on her mare and trot her out for a quick outing. But Jenks had warned her, Têtu must stick to the schedule of workouts he had prepared for her. And she was not about to spoil any efforts which would prevent a successful outcome for the race. How much had Pen exhausted Patience by having her carry two men and at such a distance last night? She hoped the rescue of her manager did not give her horse an unfair advantage.

Pen. Oh, dear Lord. When her thoughts shifted from the horses to the man, the memory of what had occurred last night between the two of them, despite her best efforts, lingered in the forefront of her mind. A longing ache dulled her senses. *I'll think about him later.*

Every one of her workers was given the day off tomorrow to attend the Ramp Festival and horse race if they so choose. And from all appearances, most of her employees not only supported the event but were excited about it as well. She smiled as she thought about the positive publicity that had been generated around the contest. Nashville was even sending down a reporter, and her attorney had fielded several calls from other newspapers enquiring about the 'Battle of the Stills' to the telephone line installed at his town office.

With happy thoughts, she twirled her key as she strolled to her office. She stopped short at her door and jerked her key away from the lock. Taped to the upper half-front glass was a piece of paper. Written in heavy black chalk was a disturbing message. *Whiskey and*

Women Don't Mix. Beware. Signed at the bottom in the same chalk was a bold black *X.*

Chloe reached up and tore the note off. With shaking hands, she unlocked her door. A sudden feeling of cold overtook her. Looking about for anyone, she did not see a soul. The hum of the whiskey mash drums sounded downstairs, no scurrying footsteps. When, and more importantly, who stuck this appalling message on her door? Was it written as a threat to her and her distillery, or was it someone who did not care for the upcoming celebration surrounding whiskey?

She stumbled inside and peered out her office window. A trio of workers, carrying their lunch buckets and chatting cheerfully, reported for the day. She did not want a repeat of when she first took control of Tanner's. She remembered her employees' anxious faces—their unease, their trepidation, and even skepticism. Did she, in truth, want to interrogate her staff to see if they had seen anything suspicious? No, not today, not one day before the race and special holiday.

"Why does this have to happen now?" she moaned out loud. Just when her employees had started to accept her, or at least appreciate how hard she worked. The last thing she intended to do was to throw a spoke in the wheel of how smooth her company was running with her at the helm. She held the repulsive piece of paper up once again to examine it. Methodically, she tore the paper in neat strips, dumping them in her wastebasket. Then, she pulled her files, and headed for the tasting room.

Chapter Seven

Where did all these people come from? If she didn't know better, she'd think Pen Kittrell had posted flyers in three counties announcing their race. Animated shouts from a rowdy crowd greeted them as they turned their wagon into the fairgrounds. Whoops, screeches, and squeals from men, women, and children surged around them. It appeared like the whole county had turned out. People swarmed en masse, soaking up the charged atmosphere, as hordes of wagons and gigs headed through the gates, making it difficult for Milo to navigate their vehicle with her horse tethered to the back.

Chloe remembered praying for rain the night before. Apparently, she hadn't prayed hard enough, as she squinted up at the cloudless sky from her seat between Jenks and Milo. Brightening, she patted Milo's back. After she came back from DC, Milo had returned to work as energetic as ever. No mention of his stomach ailment or the possibility of poisoning was ever made by him. However, the health of her favorite foreman was always at the forefront of her mind.

"We got a firm track today," he announced to her and Jenks as he assisted her down from the wagon.

She twisted the royal blue scarf, signifying their colors, tied around her waist. Bridgette insisted she wear it and had sown the same color on Bart's jersey.

Her diminutive groom had been flattered, and agreed on the spot to be her jockey in the mile-long race. Bart untied her horse from the back of the wagon and walked her through the racetrack gate to inside the fence line. Têtu whinnied and stepped back, swishing her tail with a vengeance when someone pounded a tin washtub.

Omigod. When Chloe scanned the faces belonging to those already lining the rail, she recognized several of her own workers from the distillery. Anticipation crackled through the air. Fanfare bubbled from workers from both distilleries who had looked forward to this friendly wager. Someone had tied ribbons from the finish line outward, dotting the fence line in the opposing sides' designated colors. Royal blue for Têtu and the Tanner clan and burnt-orange for Patience and the Kittrells'. Dollar bills fluttered in the air as they passed hand over hand, placing bets on their favorite.

Chloe walked along with Bart and her horse, both trying their best to keep the mare calm. It was hard not to be caught up in the excitement. Her heart soared as the cheers intensified.

"Têtu Tanner, Têtu Tanner."

"Good luck to our pretty filly," someone yelled as she passed.

She glanced around the dirt racecourse. Pen had saddled his mare and helped his jockey mount Patience and was leading her down the track away from the noise.

"Bridgette, find a place by the rail at the finish line where we can watch the race. Bart, are you ready to mount up? I want to walk over to where Pen is exercising his horse and wish him luck before the race starts."

"Yes, ma'am."

Milo gave him a leg up, checking Bart's saddle once more before delivering Têtu's backside a sound pat and hobbling away. The town's mayor caught Chloe's eye and motioned for her. Wishing to ignore him, she turned to follow Bart and her horse to where Patience was prancing.

"Miss Tanner, Miss Tanner," the town's leader called reaching her before she slipped away, his eyes dancing. "Wonderful day for a horse race. You know, there's already talk about making this an annual thing," he added with unrestrained zeal. "We could have our own little Triple Tiara race with our fillies if we could get Nashville and Shelbyville on board."

Chloe rolled her eyes upward, at the same time enjoying his enthusiasm. Feet pounded on wooden bleachers on the other side of the fence. A horn blasted from somewhere in the distance as the crowd grew louder and louder.

"Miss Tanner, if you will accompany me to the post line?" the mayor asked as he reached for Chloe's elbow. "Let's get ready to start this here race."

"I want to wish…" she started to tell the mayor when she was bumped by a group of revelers who had breached the rail line. She felt a tug on her skirt. A young woman in a pink dress with long brown curls stepped on the hem as she hurried by.

"Daisy, over here." A voice hollered from somewhere.

When Chloe looked up after checking her hem, the pink-dressed lady approached Pen. He turned and doffed his hat. They laughed at something shared between the two of them. He then encased her in a great bear hug as she in turn welcomed his embrace. Chloe watched with reluctant interest, a pang of envy, or was it jealousy that stabbed at her heart? *As if I care.*

A shout bellowed from the overflowing crowd. "Show 'em how a country filly should be ridden, Kittrell."

"I see you have brought some of your nearest and dearest friends," she said under her breath in reference to Pen as she took one more look at him before turning to search for Bridgette. The mayor had long since abandoned her to her own resources. She squeezed in behind the rail line and aimed to make her way through to the finish pole. People pushed and shoved. One or two persons appeared to recognize her and patted her back jovially. The crowd surged in anticipation of the mayor starting the race, the massive swarm rendering it almost impossible to move. A small boy hidden under a mound of dirt and a black cap, pulled her arm.

"This is for you, miss." He squashed something in her palm, then ducked, disappearing into the crowd.

In the tight press of bodies, Chloe struggled to open the folded missive. Scrawled on the scrape of paper was a large black X. Shocked, she dropped the note. Stamping feet crowding around her crumbled it to shreds in seconds.

"Never thought there'd be this much interest in a friendly wager." Pen's voice penetrated the clamor.

Chloe swayed toward him. Her heartbeat muffled the surrounding sounds.

"Is something the matter?" he asked, studying her face.

"I'm not real good with crowds," she confessed, as

raucous participants jammed in tighter, slapping their back and shoulders. *And please, please let that note be somebody's sick prank.*

"I've got you." Pen secured her with a strong arm and shepherded her to the track's edge. "Let me take you over to the pole."

She gripped his sturdy limb as he muscled them through the throng of onlookers to reach the finish line marker.

"Ladies and Gentlemen of Oak Hollow. May I have your attention please." The mayor stood on a wooden platform, waving the streamer high as a gust of wind blew across the track. "Welcome to our first ever Filly Fling. I will start the race with the drop of this yellow flag and one shot from the starting pistol. Racers are at their posts. Are you ready?" he yelled.

Chloe placed her hand on her hammering heart, tension mingled with excitement streamed through her. "I guess it's time."

"On your mark." The yellow flag dropped as a gunshot blasted. Both horses bolted headlong.

The crowd surged forward, pressing Chloe against the rails. Pen moved behind her, enabling her to breathe. She clasped his arm just as the horses passed the quarter mile. A lightness in her chest returned and she joined in the excitement. Bridgette had somehow found her and squeezed into a half-inch spot, gripping her hand tight.

"Têtu's winning. She's ahead," her maid squealed.

Feeling like her insides vibrated, Chloe pressed her fist to her mouth as her horse took easy strides allowing Bart to turn Têtu comfortably at the half-mile marker. Both horses' beautiful, muscled bodies gleamed in the midday sun. And neither horse seemed winded. Was Pen letting her horse win? His jockey had not tapped Patience once with his whip.

On the backstretch, Chloe's horse turned her head, the act was akin to seeing if the fellow equine was still with her, and at that point, her filly slowed. Was her horse waiting for the new friend to catch up? The crowd howled its approval as Patience pulled alongside Têtu. The two horses galloped around the last quarter-mile neck and neck.

A deafening roar rose from the throng as Patience, who apparently had no patience, decided she had had enough and stretched for the finish line to win it all, beating Têtu by a head.

Chloe felt the strong arms encircling her draw away. She turned and ducked before getting hit by a boot as two brawny men lifted Pen to their shoulders and carried him to the track with an entourage of happy racegoers following. Someone thrust a burnt-orange scarf in her hand and nudged her through the rail opening to join them. Pen, smiling above the multitude, tried to keep his balance, grasping the shoulders of the frenzied pack holding him. Once he spotted her, he leaned over begging the two human cranes to lower him.

"Better go give him the winning colors, so as we can head home," Milo hollered in her ear.

"First, I want to thank Bart." She scampered across the dirt track to meet her horse and jockey. She caught Têtu's bridle and patted her beloved horse's mane.

"Miss Chloe, I'm sorry I didn't win."

"Oh no, Bart. You and Têtu gave us a marvelous race." She laid her head against her mare. "I couldn't be more proud."

"Looks like a lot of other folks feel the same way," her jockey said as he slipped from his mount.

She looked toward the bleachers. Most of the crowd had dispersed, but along the rail stood a line of her employees waving their royal blue banners, beaming, waiting to praise their distillery's owner and her horse.

"Têtu Tanner, Têtu Tanner!" People shouted.

"Still the prettiest filly in the county, and the one with the biggest heart."

"You do us proud, Miss Tanner. Nice of you to let Kittrell's come in first for once."

"Thank you, thank you." Smiling, she walked to the rail. She shook extended hands until her fingers grew numb and her arm hurt, laughing at their jokes and accepting their well-wishes. Her lungs expanded. A rush of relief flooded through her. As the men lifted their hats, she raised her chin in acknowledgment and smiled back.

The small gathering at mid-track around Pen had separated, making a path for her to surrender the ribbon. She pushed herself in his direction, never taking her eyes off him. *He's helping me.* If I just concentrate on his face, one step at a time, I can do this. She reached his outstretched arm and lifted his winning colors for him. He waved the streamer a second above his head, then slid down his supporter's shoulders.

"Kiss the winner," someone cried out from close range.

The heat of the day, the shoving back and forth of the jam-packed crowd, the note, and the exuberant shouts from the townsfolk and her employees coalesced, overwhelming her. He took her hands in his and pulled her to him. She pressed a quick kiss to the side of his mouth to appease the spirited onlookers before sagging against his hard body.

"Clear away, clear away. Let a person breathe now," Pen bade the bystanders. "First round drinks on me at O'Malley's. Let's celebrate."

"Woo Hoo." The boisterous swarm pumped their fists and waved their arms.

"Great race," Milo barked his approval. "Folks, let us get these horses taken care of."

The agreeable crowd scattered. Happy to claim their winnings and recount their opinions, they hurried away to lift a toast to the victor with their free shots of whiskey.

"Come on, Milo's right. Let's get these fillies rubbed down and returned to their stables," Pen said without releasing her.

As Bridgette and Milo went to help Bart and Jenks, Pen gave her shoulder a gentle squeeze. "You going to be all right?"

"Yes, thank you. And congratulations," she replied, her eyes brimming with happiness. "I thought Têtu was going to win. I had no idea she was so sociable. Just wanting to be with her newfound friend."

"I thought both horses gave us and the whole town an incredible race. And uh—" He looked down at her expectantly. "—I've picked the perfect spot. I think we should picnic tomorrow by the little lake on the edge of your property."

"Well, you won fair and square. Bridgette and I will meet you there at noon."

He chuckled, giving her a sideways glance.

"You didn't think I would come alone, did you?"
"No, of course not."

Chapter Eight

"Mr. Kittrell seems like a nice gentleman."

Chloe rolled her eyes, pulling the curricle to a stop by her property's little lake.

"Bridgette, don't tell me you've fallen under the Kittrell Spell?" She fluffed the lace collar of her lavender Indian silk shirtwaist. She chose the silk dress instead of the gingham Bridgette first laid out for her because the color embodied her high spirits. The violet shade complimented her face and hair coloring much better. A fact she noted when she took a last glance in the cheval mirror before leaving her bedroom earlier this morning.

A soft breeze blew across the meadow on the near-perfect day, lifting Chloe's new hat. She captured an errant tendril and curled it around her ear. The new wide-brimmed confection trimmed with fluttering green ribbons and cream-colored blossoms, another excellent choice, allowed her to drive unhindered and leave her parasol behind.

"No, ma'am. But I believe he has eyes on you," her maid ventured, her cornflower blue eyes peeking from under her bonnet.

"Humph. He's our competition. Our sworn enemy in business. Don't you forget it." *And that's the only world I can operate under right now.* "Yesterday was fun, though," she admitted. And she was looking forward to today, deciding to dismiss the recent disturbing messages as some kind of harebrained prank.

"I'm starving. If he doesn't show up soon, we'll eat lunch without him. There's two baskets packed," she said as she glanced in the back of her rig. "We can take one and give him the other."

Horse's hoofbeats sounded from the other side of the honeysuckle hedgerow, Pen and another rider trotted through the opening. As they got closer, she recognized one of the McCoy triplets.

Bridgette grabbed her arm. "He's brought Corbin."

"No, that's Caleb, his brother. You know, Corbin and Caleb are identical twins—Clark is the triplet who's not." Chloe revealed.

"No, I didn't know," Bridgette said as she stared.

"Good afternoon, ladies. Was beginning to think we were the only folks about today—not a soul in town. Appears like the whole county tied one on yesterday and is taking the day off."

Pen jumped down from his horse and looked in the back of Chloe's gig before helping her down. He lifted one basket out and gathered a blanket stuffed under the driver's seat. "Caleb, tie Patience to Miss Tanner's curricle. You can take her around with you to the other side of the lake. We're picnicking over by the big oak." He gingerly took her arm and walked toward a shaded area.

"I should have known you'd have a distraction for my lady's maid," Chloe said after watching Bridgette succumb to Pen's directions. "Can't believe you'd bring the twin of the man she's sweet on."

"Spoken from the lips of the woman who poached my manager in training away from me using a similar tactic."

"Touché."

"By the way—I do want to request a ride in your curricle sometime—word is, you drive like the devil."

Chloe laughed as she spread the quilt under the giant oak. "Have you ever had the man from Beecher Cardboard call on you?"

"Once or twice."

"Well, then you know I needed a way to be rid of him. It took me just two turns around my track."

"Chloe, for shame." He chuckled. After he placed their basket on the blanket, he started removing its contents. "Lemonade," he said as he pulled out the drink jar. "No wine? Ahh, someone in the kitchen at Tanner house must like me." He lifted a whiskey pint tucked in under the napkins.

"You're incorrigible. Let's eat," she said as she untied her hat.

"This is delicious. Do you cook?"

"Some."

"What's your best recipe?"

"French Toast."

"Which I love," he said, laughing again. "By the way, I was thinking I should have let you win the horse race yesterday. My bar bill from O'Malley's almost broke the bank."

"Oh, pooh. Let me win. It was all you could do to overcome my horse. And you'll get no sympathy from me. I saw the exchange boards last time I was upstairs at the courthouse. By the way, credit to you for installing them for us, looks like the pictures I've seen of the cotton exchange in Memphis."

"That's what gave me the idea. Speaking of

exchange boards. I see your company is recovering rather well. My compliments for handling the Tanner reins for whiskey as well as horses," he said holding a cup up in a toast. "McCoy says his brother declares you are quite the even-handed boss. Don't play favorites, like he says he thought a woman in charge would."

"Should I take that as a compliment?" she mocked.

"Yes." He studied her eyes as if trying to read them. "By the way, how is your general manager recovering?"

"Fine, he's doing fine." Her cheeks prickled, seeking to maintain her composure and not reveal her emotions about what had transpired between the two of them in the moonlight a mere four days earlier. "Speaking of the McCoy's, Corbin thanked me for treating him as an individual," she disclosed trying to move the subject in another direction. "He likes when I call him by his first name. Said he wasn't too sure you ever could tell him and his brother's apart."

"Well, they're triplets."

"He said that was one of the reasons he came to work for me. Pen, your father was a hard taskmaster. Maybe you think you have to be tough like him in order to succeed, but getting to know your employees, sharing a little of yourself with them, doesn't mean you're weak."

"I wasn't planning on running a whiskey distillery either. In fact, I more or less ran away from it for a year. But I guess it was in my blood, kinda like you. Hard to give up." He studied her face before adding, "Point well taken, about the employees by the way."

After making quick work of the basket's contents, Pen finished his drink while watching Chloe stretch her legs, smoothing her silk skirt over her limbs. Moving closer to her, he laid beside her and propped himself up on his elbow.

"Isn't this the time during the picnic where I get to lay back in your lap and take a nap?"

"Obviously, you didn't attend the picnics I did in Boston."

"No," he replied then reached out and took her hand. "Have you ever had your fortune told?"

"And have the teller whisper to me I'll meet a tall, dark, and handsome stranger?" she derided. "That ship has sailed."

"Are you saying I'm handsome?" He sat up, studying her.

"You are so conceited," she said as she tried to pull her hand away.

He turned her hand over and ran his thumb across her palm. "If your fate line starts at your lifeline, see this is your fate line"—he stroked the outer edge of her hand—"and this is your lifeline, it means you've had a strong sense of purpose since birth."

Mesmerized, she allowed him to hold her hand while rubbing his long fingers across the contours on her palm.

"If your heart line is wavy, it indicates several lovers."

She struggled to pull her hand away to peek at her palm herself, but he held fast. "You won't let me see if I have many lovers?"

"No." He ignored her and continued, "If your heartline and headline run parallel it means…"

"I've heard enough, you can't tell…" She freed her hand at last.

"Some people don't have a heartline, but you do, I saw it. And it tells me…" He reached up sliding his hand behind her head. He drew her closer to his face, running his thumb down her cheek and jaw, "Chloe." He tilted his head. "Let me kiss you."

She didn't pull away. She let his lips graze hers, then moved into his arms for a deep kiss.

Chloe placed her hands on his shoulders, then with regret pushed him away. "No, Pen. We can't. Mustn't."

"Are you worried about McCoy? He won't come unless I call him," he said hoarsely.

"No. You know this can never happen again. We can't." She shook her head. "Oh, I can't explain it." A blue jay flew overhead, his harsh cawing breaking the spell.

He withdrew.

The mood or moment had passed. She thought he'd be the type of man not to press his interest if the other participant didn't hold mutual feelings.

Grabbing his hat from the blanket, he twirled it a minute as if in contemplation then placed it on her head. "Take good care of it. I've got to cool off. I'm going for a swim."

He leaned over and removed his boots and socks, then stood and unbuttoned his shirt tugging it off. Chloe scooted to the edge of the blanket and watched. As he grasped his belt buckle, he gave a sideways glance. "Want to join me?" he asked unbuckling his belt and sliding off his trousers.

"No. Go ahead. Be my guest." She inhaled, trying to catch her breath as he stripped off his undershirt, leaving on his knee-length cotton drawers.

He strode across the grass and plunged into the

cool water, diving under.

"Feels great, you don't know what you're missing," he hollered as he surfaced. He made smooth and easy strokes through the water, laughing as he performed deep dives, then re-emerged in a different spot. He waded into shallower waters then sent a splash her way. "Last chance."

She ought to turn her head, or better yet, pretend to pack up the basket, but she couldn't. How beautiful he looked unclothed, sinfully gorgeous. Water droplets glimmered over his body. His shoulders, chest, arms, and torso. Miles of muscle. *Heavens above.* As he treaded water toward the shore, her gaze dipped to below his waistline, his soaked underwear might as well be transparent. In less than two feet of water, he beckoned her again to join him by splashing water up to the shore.

"Hang on. I'm coming in." Never had she behaved so uninhibited and spontaneous. Unabashed, she stood and started unbuttoning her dress and kicking off her shoes when an explosion pierced the air. She yelped and clutched her chest, staggering to retain her balance as a muffled reverberation shook the ground.

Pen stopped in the knee-high water and turned in the direction of the blast. Another enormous detonation punctured their idyllic surroundings. He scampered out of the water, jerking his clothes on over his wet body.

"What was that?" Chloe gasped as she attempted to slide her shoes on.

"Don't know. But it's come from the direction of your distillery."

Chapter Nine

"Sweet Jesus, what happened?" Chloe flung picnic remnants in the basket.

"Leave it." Pen grabbed her arm and they ran to the opening in the honeysuckle hedge toward the wagon path. "McCoy, McCoy!" he shouted. "Over here."

Chloe searched the valley but trees obscured her sight. She gazed up at the sky, hoping to see gray clouds that signaled a brewing storm. Blue as far as she saw.

The cart hurtled down the dirt pathway, but for her liking, still too slow. Bridgette hung onto Caleb as he whipped the horses to a bounding gait. Strapped behind the curricle were both his and Pen's horses.

"Caleb, untie your pinto for Miss Tanner. She needs to get to Tanner Place fast." Caleb jumped out and untied his horse. Pen grabbed Patience's reins. "Follow in the gig. Up you go, Chloe." Pen caught Chloe's waist and threw her astride Caleb's western saddle, the flurry of bunched white petticoats exposed her bare limb. He pushed her foot in the stirrups. "Are you secure on the other side?"

"Yes." Her hands shook. Was it her house, the stables…the distillery? She pulled tight on the bridle. *Oh, my Lord.* The note. Was what was happening connected to the threat taped to her office door two days ago? Was this 'X's' doing?

"All right, let's ride." Pen mounted his horse, kicked Patience's flanks, and set a frenzied pace. In minutes, he cut off the beaten path and galloped across the heather pasture, and then charged through the ripening cornfield.

Acrid smoke reached Chloe as they crested the ridge. She forced her gaze off Pen's back and looked skyward. A plume of gray smoke snaked its way over the blue horizon. Dear God. She jerked back on the bridle. There was no way the smoke could come from anywhere else but her distillery. Her heartbeat raced. She wished she could turn away. A sense of impending doom crashed into her.

"Almost there." Pen urged their horses on.

Thank God he was with her. But if she hadn't been on this senseless picnic. Unfair. She had been looking forward to a time where the two of them could finally come to terms or at least sort out their relationship. But saints above, she should have been at home where she could help. Or be killed. Her mother? Oh, my lord. Please, God. Her heart stopped.

She muttered a silent prayer before giving her mount an urgent kick. They galloped down the hill crossways through Regina's orchard and garden, racing toward the stable. Horses ran past them. They pulled up short in the stable yard. Both barn doors swung wide. Someone had opened the stalls and freed the animals.

"Quick thinking," Pen said springing from his horse.

Burning wood permeated the hot air and crackling came from somewhere behind a veil of smoke hiding her distillery from view. Gray figures emerged from a lifting vaporized curtain like a scene from Dante's

Inferno carrying buckets as they trudged up the slope to the barn's waterspout.

"More water," someone shouted.

"Form a line." She overheard her head groom shout as a ribbon of bodies linked arm to bucket, bucket to arm.

Chloe dismounted and stood next to Pen, transfixed by the clearing scene fifty yards away. The whole front of her distillery's structure had collapsed. Now, nothing was left but a pile of brick and lumber. The entire second floor pancaked the lower floor in the most damaged section. Flames wicked their way through the ravaged roofline and splotches of fireballs had landed as far away as the stable rooftop. Jutting out from the remaining outer walls were pieces of wood thrown like darts against a dartboard. Dangling dangerously from the rooftop over the front eave was their century-old weathervane. A giant smoke waft billowed over the destruction, filling her nostrils, making her eyes water.

"Dear, God." She fisted her hand to her mouth as she viewed the spectacle before her. *I'm glad Grandpa is not here to see this.*

A crash of collapsing timber startled her. Pen swore above the deafening chaos.

A woman called for a loved one.

"We need more buckets!"

"Fetch more water! Need it on the west side," shouted a voice Chloe recognized.

"Go get the buckets and tubs from the washhouse." She grabbed the arm of her youngest groom and directed him toward the main house.

"Was anyone hurt? Has everyone been accounted for?" she pleaded as one of her workers passed. He shook his head.

"Need help over here."

"Found someone!"

She stepped over piles of debris. Broken glass crunched beneath her feet.

"Watch where you step," Pen warned, leaving her. He raced to the group of men straining to raise a wooden timber off a rubble pile.

"Wait, I'm coming." Forcing her gaze from the madness before her, she picked her way through the wreckage. She slipped in the thick soot covering the yard between the stable and distillery, falling hard on her backside. She stood, yanked the hem of her dress from a fallen board, tearing it.

"Anyone under there?" Pen yelled. She reached his side. He drew a quick breath of relief. The bloody, dirty person pulled from beneath the rubble raised his head. She uttered a small, choked cry. He's alive. Oh please, let him be the only one injured. Let no one else be hurt.

Two men plodded over the bricks carrying one of the factory doors. Rescuers loaded the man on the makeshift stretcher. Her bookkeeper.

"It's Hector," she whispered, shock paralyzing her. As they lifted him, his right arm slipped, and she caught sight of his hand. A bloody mangled mess. Her stomach retched. Bending over, she placed her hands on her knees and gave in to dry heaves. Milo spotted her and hobbled over and patted her back.

"I'm okay," she said straightening, her knees still wobbling.

"No one else in the building, just Hector. Thank God, he was upstairs in his office, instead of down below." He shook his head. "They located Virgil first, he's alive but unconscious," he said with a pained expression. "Damn lucky. Must have been standing in the doorway. Blast blew him clear away. We found him lying by the big cedar."

Careful to avoid broken boards, she climbed over the rubble and addressed the rescuers. "Take Hector to the annex." She beckoned the woman she saw earlier. "Darlene, help show them the way. And someone send for a doctor." She rubbed her eyes and looked about again. "Darlene, find my mother, too. She can help you."

She spied Bart in a line of half a dozen people staring at her, their eyes glazed over in a daze, and motioned to him. "Go over to the stable barn and climb up the back and try to put those sparks out—can't afford to lose our barn too."

The other men listened as she gave orders. "Mark the vats which aren't damaged. Everything has got to be secured or destroyed. We can't have anyone accusing us of contamination."

Corbin McCoy exited from the hole blasted open by the explosion and trudged over to her, Milo, and Pen. "We're lucky. The tank nearest the explosion was full and the contents ran down the factory proper and put out any startup fires."

"What do you think happened?" Pen asked.

"Not sure. Don't understand it. Ain't nothing combustible in this end of the plant," he said as he kicked a piece of burned wood out of the way.

"Dynamite. Had to be. Nothing else that powerful," Milo declared.

"Did you have dynamite on the premises?" Corbin asked, turning to both Milo and Chloe.

"No," answered Milo. "Don't need it. And just about impossible to get anyhow. When Federal troops were still in charge during Reconstruction, they got tired of chasing down disturbances. Passed a law—making it so all purchases had to be approved in Nashville."

"Didn't you use dynamite last spring to blow up some rock?" Corbin questioned Pen.

"Yeah. We had to blow up a boulder so we could pipe in more cooling water. Still have some left."

Chloe stepped back, stumbling over bits of broken mortar and bricks, hearing Pen's admission. Glancing about to see what others might think of this disclosure, she inhaled. She couldn't imagine the power it would take to destroy a boulder. Well, if it was dynamite, it had without a doubt done a job on her distillery.

She scanned the perimeter of her distillery once again. The clearing smoke revealed an even worse picture of the scope of the calamity. Wood splinters the size of railroad ties were strewn everywhere, rubble from the factory's stone foundation heaped in piles like someone's tossed out pillows. She tasted the cordite and black powder still burning in the hot air, yet she shivered. Her skin felt cold and clammy, her pulse nonexistent, her throat parched.

She wiped the back of her hand over her eyes and watched as the score of workers along with their wives and children sorted through the wreckage. Her distillery. Their distillery. If the explosion was not an accident...? Hoping no one noticed her hands trembling, she pretended to shake a spark from her dress. *I can't, I can't be going into shock now. I've got to hold it together.* After another deep breath, she stared at the three men in front of her. She dared to ask out loud what they were thinking. "Who would do such a thing, why, and when?"

"Don't know." Corbin shuffled a boot in the inch-deep soot. "But it takes a while to set charges."

" 'Spec the work was done while we was at the race," Milo stated.

For a minute, no one in the group spoke. She thought she glimpsed something like sympathy, or was it guilt in Pen's expression?

"So why not blow the place up yesterday?" Corbin asked the obvious.

"Maybe got interrupted or maybe planned all along for it to go off today. If this here explosion took place yesterday, you'd eliminate the whole county as suspects. Makes it harder this way," Milo answered.

"But wouldn't Hector or Virgil see who set it? They were here today," Chloe asked.

"Nah, more likely whoever did this used a bow and torched arrow then shot at a haybale sitting on a powder trail. Safer that way," Milo added.

Chloe's eyes widened at the revelation. Fear growled at her like some wild animal deep in the woods. "Well, let's help get this place cleaned up," she said as she wiped her blackened hands on her silk lavender dress. "Plenty of time to figure everything out tomorrow," she said with more confidence than she felt. And plenty of time to wonder who would do this.

"I better get back to my distillery and check on it," Pen said to the group, taking his leave.

"Better stop by the sheriff's office on your way back and let him know what happened here. He'll want to come over straight away to investigate," Milo said.

"The sheriff?" Pen and Chloe asked.

"Sure. From the looks of it—someone did this on purpose. If that's so, it'll be a crime."

****

Pen hesitated. His fingers rested on the safe's combination lock. What would he find? He hoped his suspicions were unfounded, but he'd not bet on it. He glanced over his shoulder then focused. He had to be certain. He turned the dial, the year of his birth. In all probability a slew of babies born that year. Nine months after the majority of men in the south tramped off to war. One, turn, eight, turn, six, click back, and two, click back again. The lock released and Pen opened the huge walk-in safe. He entered, leaving Caleb on the other side of the solid steel door.

One burlap sack was tossed in the corner. Empty. Enough dynamite to blow a hole in another five-ton boulder of granite, gone.

"McCoy, guess you better be a witness, ain't no explosives in here." Pen stepped aside and let his foreman enter. "Did we hire anyone new since I went to DC?"

"No, we haven't hired anybody new since last year," Caleb answered. "Nobody enters here 'cept me and the bookkeeper when we pass out wages. We meet our salesmen downstairs like always. Every now and then, a gypsy from Piney Flats comes by the yard, you think it might be one of them?"

"No, I don't. It doesn't appear any money is missing," Pen closed the giant cashbox which sat on the first shelf. "How about anything suspicious happening in the yards?"

"Nope. But your window was broken last month

when you were in Cincinnati," Caleb said as he walked over to it. "Looked like a bird hit it, more like a rock. Forgot about that. We had a glazer come in and fix it."

Pen ran his hand across the glass pane then trudged back over to his safe. "If someone were to put a piece of glass in the lock's hole pocket, could the door still close?"

"Yeah, boss, but the door wouldn't lock."

"But if it were closed, wouldn't you assume it was locked? Thinking maybe the bookkeeper locked it?" Looking around once again he ran his fingers through his hair. "Dynamite. Do you remember hearing about a distillery up north getting blown up last year?"

"Yeah, in Chicago."

"Rumor was there was some unofficial 'trust' trying to buy up distilleries to control price and quantity and someone refused to enter the combine. But Oak Hollow is not Chicago where every other person you meet is a stranger. There's just one rail track coming in and out of here, be darn difficult to pull something big off without some local help. Regardless, I don't want to be next. I want a night watchman hired straightway to keep an eye on this place while we're not here." He looked inside the safe again at the empty shelf, then exhaled, "I guess we'll never know for sure who took it. I better report this theft to the sheriff. Don't know what he'll think."

Don't know what she'll think. Would she straight up imagine he had a part in blowing up her distillery and injuring two innocent employees in the process? Hell, if she credited half of the stories of some of his pa's exploits, she'd have reason to believe he was capable of it.

"Speaking of gypsies, I think I'll ride over to Piney Flats tomorrow. Haven't been there in a while." He'd ask Fatima if she had heard of any suspicious persons hanging about.

****

The smell of burned wood and smoke permeated the air. Loose dangling shingles and boards protruded from the factory's rafters, shattered debris poked out of weeping siding, and spilled whiskey mash from yesterday's wreckage oozed like a raw wound from her distillery. Chloe walked through a path of splintered wood and crumbled brick and stone. The narrow walkway cleared by her league of employees and family members who had worked alongside her deep into the night to make some semblance of order to her severely damaged distillery.

For the first time Chloe could remember, she had risen early and raced to the plant, not to oversee the tastings of the last batch of whiskey, but to see if what she witnessed yesterday was real. Any hope it had been a bad dream was met with grueling reality. Someone had perpetrated a horrific, almost fatal, crime against Tom Tanner's Tennessee Whiskey. She swallowed hard. The burn of bile gulped down her throat. *Who, why?*

Corbin McCoy wandered from around the rear of the damaged building. "Miss Tanner?"

"Yes, Corbin?" He was still sporting the remnants of a black eye from his fight at the Red Bruin. How long ago that seemed.

"Sheriff's inside the distillery now. Came by to get a first look at things. A wee bit of good news, well, I hope we can save the bottling machine. Even though the device was in the middle of the impact, a ceiling beam and roofing fell on it, protecting it from flying debris. Won't know for sure until later." He stubbed his toe in the soot covering the ground then looked up. "Miss Tanner, when I went home last night, Caleb told me Pen Kittrell's dynamite was gone."

"Gone?" She slammed her hands on her hips. *Really Pen. How could something so dangerous go missing, and you not know it?*

"Says it was stolen. Someone went to some trouble to get it."

"How so?"

"It wasn't kept in a storeroom at the warehouse. The sticks were kept in his safe. A walk-in safe with a huge combination lock on it." He shook his head. "No one had the combination 'cept him and his bookkeeper."

"Makes no sense." All distilleries were on guard for theft. Mostly for their product, their precious yeast recipes, but also for payroll and anything else valuable. Hard to believe Kittrell's would be any different. For a moment Corbin stood and surveyed the damage with her before they both turned to greet the sheriff walking toward them.

"Good morning, Sheriff."

"Miss Tanner." He removed his hat. "Looks like you have a hell of a mess in there, excuse my language."

"I would have to agree with you."

"Most probably was dynamite. We'll know for certain when we test this dry powder. Been talking to some of the other county sheriffs close by and everyone's having dust-ups with the temperance people. But what I can't figure out is why the explosion damaged more of your equipment and office stuff than actual alcohol. Not what them temperance people are out to destroy. Appears like most of your barrels of whiskey are intact." He cocked his head in the direction of her barrel warehouse. "Do you have any reason to suspect anyone of doing this? Any threats?"

She struggled to conceal her anguish. Too late to tell him about the threatening note. He'd think she was an absolute nitwit to have thrown it away. Avoiding eye contact, she crossed her arms and walked down the path, then paused. "Milo Knox told me last night, he thought this deed was meant to be a warning. Someone's inexperience with dynamite most likely caused a much bigger explosion than planned. That the intention was to not cause this much damage or harm anyone."

"If it were not anyone's intention to do this much damage, I'd hate to see what would have happened if it was. Well, I'll be in touch. You take care now."

She thanked the sheriff. She waved Corbin over. "To me, Corbin, this signals someone wants Tom Tanner Whiskey. Well, they are not going to get it. And you can tell that to your brothers, so I can be sure the message gets back to Mr. Penland Kittrell."

She walked on, pointing up to the blown-off rooftop. "I had planned on modernizing this plant. What occurred yesterday, just prompts me to go ahead a little earlier with my ideas. I think I will buy at least three more bottling machines. I can build a separate assembly building, where bottling and labeling take place away from the production of whiskey and add more brewing tanks to the factory proper and construct more rick houses."

"Miss Tanner, what you're proposing will take a whole heap of money."

"Yes, it will. We have some insurance, not much. But I can raise money through the sale of stock." She glanced over at the gurgling stream below the damaged structure. "We still have our water. No one's destroyed that."

Chapter Ten

"Well, who have we here?" A little boy with soft brown curls and big hazel eyes peeped out from behind one of the storage vats as Chloe turned to ascend the stairs to her office. He ducked shyly behind the container as a woman appeared from the same direction.

"Miss Tanner?"

Chloe turned around. "Raelynn, it is you, isn't it?"

"Yes."

"Is this your little boy?" she asked before she noticed Raelynn Brown wore no wedding band.

"Yes, his name is Dillon, after my grandfather."

"Come upstairs, if you have time, I have some butterscotch drops."

"I came to get some of Hector's things, Miss Tanner."

"Call me Chloe, you've known me too long, Raelynn. How is your brother?"

"Well, that's one of the things I come to talk to you about." The two women turned and climbed the stairs as the sheriff walked through the north distillery door with Corbin McCoy. Chloe stopped.

"Raelynn, you go on ahead. You know which office was your brother's. I'll be upstairs in a minute."

Chloe proffered her hand to the sheriff, whom she'd spoken to a week earlier. "Sheriff."

"Miss Tanner, I'm sorry, I'm bringing some unpleasant news. It was definitely dynamite that blew up your distillery. And as of yet, we have no suspects for what I'd call out and out sabotage."

Chloe eyes widened as a sensation of ice water flowing through her veins battered her numb body. Yes, she had suspected this news, but hearing it from the sheriff was different. Taking two steps back, she scanned Corbin's face for any doubt. None was there.

"Any clues at all?" she asked.

"Only dynamite around here belonged to Pen Kittrell, and he's reported his stolen. Have to ask, but do you know of anyone who'd want to damage your distillery? Didn't you fire a manager a short time ago?"

"That man, I can assure you, Sheriff, would not step a foot in this county again. Especially if it did not involve him receiving money. Never met a more dishonest or greedier man."

"Well, one thing we do know is—them temperance people have some vigilantes in their corner. Bunches of them around. They's crazy folks, Miss Tanner, I wouldn't put anything past them. You let me know, Miss, if you receive any threats or God forbid anything else happens out here."

After the sheriff left, Corbin detained her. "Miss Tanner, we had three distillery people come by this morning. Wanted to offer help. We could use any lumber they have. It would help."

"Who were they?"

"Dawson's, Murray's, and Kittrell's.

"Don't take anything from Kittrell's. I don't care what they offer." She turned, leaving her dumbfounded manager at the base of the stairs.

He wouldn't dare! Pen Kittrell, you wouldn't dare. She started up the stairs to the offices above, glancing again at the gaping hole in part of her roof. For once, she was thankful for the lack of rain. So, it was dynamite and no one else in the county or beyond had any except Pen. How convenient the explosion took place on a Sunday, and no one was at the plant or should have been. And she was away on a picnic of all things.

She pounded the guardrail so hard her hand stung. The simmering rage in her body exploded. Why, oh why? Of the entire population of men on this earth she could have made love to did she have to pick him? The hurt, the pain. The shocking realization that she had been betrayed by the man who thoughts of kept her up at night hit home.

Your plant is doing quite well this quarter. Pen's words echoed through her brain. He had to be behind the dynamiting. Was he trying to eliminate her as a competitor? Or was it a warning, a scare tactic, like those awful notes. A deed which far exceeded the damage than intended. Squeezing her eyes shut, she shook her hand, rubbing her tender palm. Would he dare do such a thing? Her lips curled. *I will not stop until I find out who did this.*

When she reached the landing, she walked into her office and grabbed a handful of butterscotchs before heading to the accountant's office. Raelynn was there with the little boy still holding tightly to his mother's skirt.

"If your mother says it's okay, I brought you some candy." She smiled down at the child before looking back at Raelynn.

"Thank you. Dillon, go see what you can spot from the window from up here," she said as she passed her son a piece. She stood wringing her wrists a moment, then raised clear eyes to Chloe. "Miss Chloe, it's doubtless that my brother is going to regain use of his hand. And you see, without his salary, things will be mighty hard this year. I count on his income to support me and Dillon."

"Raelynn, did you not get the compensation money we sent?"

"Yes, yes I did. And it will help. It's just, with Hector not working, well, I thought I could work. And my brother's agreed to mind Dillon for me."

"That's an excellent idea."

"I'm glad you think so, because I want to come work for you."

"For me?"

"Yes, I want to take Hector's position. I took a year of secretarial school after high school. Did you know that?"

"No, I didn't."

"And right after your grandpa and Noah passed," her voice wavered, "after they passed and you was up north, I came over and helped Hector with the books. I know I can do his job."

"I see. And I'm sure you're well qualified, but his position was more complicated than just bookkeeping."

"No disrespect, Miss Tanner, but I look around your distillery, and I see you're the only woman working here. How do you think these men judge a woman boss if they don't see another woman in the plant doing any of the jobs here, 'cept the one whose inherited from her grandpa?"

Chloe stood and looked out her office window, then went to the door and stepped out. Scanning the scene below, a sight which always made her blood pulse more intently, made her heart beat stronger, she looked at with different eyes. She saw what Raelynn saw. Plenty of able-bodied men, but not one single woman. She turned and walked back in the office.

"You're right, Raelynn. I'll hire you," she said decisively. "Right now, I've got a man my lawyer sent from Nashville helping as a temporary arrangement. He can start training you. Or maybe you can show him a thing or two. When can you start?"

****

Later that evening, Chloe wandered through her mother's sitting room. There, on top of the crocheted table covering, were the pictures of her and her brother. She picked up one photo. It was of Noah, seemingly a similar age as Raelynn's little boy. He wasn't just similar. He was the spitting image of Noah.

Could it be possible? Yes, more than possible. Any red-blooded man would be attracted to the lovely and sweet young woman from Bald Gap. Would Raelynn ever tell her she was her little boy's aunt? They were proud people down there. Poor as church mice, but stubbornly proud. If my mother were stronger, I'd see she met the little boy. *If Mother saw him, she'd know. Well, for now at least I've given the little boy's mother a job.*

She trudged up to her bedroom, moving across the room to her washstand. She lifted the pitcher and poured water into the shallow basin. As she splashed cold water on her face, she caught her reflection in the mirror. When had she lost her chubby cheeks? She thought she'd never get rid of them. A woman's face stared back at her. Dark crescent circles stood out in her translucent face. She wiped away the moisture with a dry cloth. Her hand lingered on her cheek. Had she transformed so much in the past months?

Could anyone look at her and tell she'd had a lover? Or would they think the strain of running such a huge company and dealing with a suspicious explosion, which tore through her factory almost killing two workers, had dealt a blow to her appearance? The muscles in her body numbed. She squeezed her eyes shut. She could still see the mangled hand of her bookkeeper and the destruction to her distillery. *Please, please I beg of you, Lord.* She prayed no other innocent would be hurt because of hostility toward her.

With the sheriff confirming today the source of her distillery's explosion, the devastation took on a whole new meaning. She opened the top drawer of her bureau chest. There below her stockings and garters she pulled out a letter she found the first day she had returned from Washington.

After firing her general manager, she had scoured every inch of Jed Sanders' office searching for incriminating evidence. Scrubbed clean in her mind, except for one sheet of letterhead stationery from Penland Kittrell Distributors left conveniently with a few other papers in his desk drawer. It was a brief note from Pen to Sanders dated a year before, thanking him for agreeing to the new project and looking forward to working together on its completion.

Chloe read the letter again, rubbing her finger across Pen's signature. She'd never seen his handwriting before. This signature was sure and strong.

Just like she thought he was. But how well did she know Pen? And what was the project they referred to? She had taken the letter and hid it. Not sure why, but for whatever reason, did not want it in the hands of others. Could Sanders have left this innocent piece of correspondence behind to have her suspect Pen?

She pulled a note from her pocket given to her this morning. It was also from Pen, asking to meet him tomorrow. The hand delivered message, passed to her as she walked from her house by a stable hand, had not been a complete surprise. He aspired to declare his innocence she figured, since word was out about his dynamite missing.

Whether Pen was behind it all or not, she didn't know. If she were still in Boston, she would hire a private investigator. But she was unable to forget that Pen asked her to marry him when they were in DC. Not because he loved her. But because he could take all her burdens away, he said. And she had a ton of burdens now. How convenient.

Made sense. More sense than the other theory bandied about. Did anyone think those passive temperance people would blow up a building? Not on your life. If they were going to destroy anything it'd be the huge vats of alcohol being produced, not the bookkeepers' office.

She tossed the letter back in the drawer on top of another letter she had not discarded. This one from her aunt insisting she return to Boston. Her aunt's strident black cursive handwriting left no doubt, with pure admonishment, of the mess Chloe had 'embroiled' herself in. It was time for her to take her 'proper place in society,' not playact as a manager of a distillery. The missive closed with the hint suggesting if she continued to spurn Peter Tanner, that Massachusetts's newly elected bachelor senator had asked about her at a recent function, and it might be promising to renew his acquaintance. *Wonderful, now I've lost support from my own family.*

Did anyone not question her? Did anyone believe in her?

Chapter Eleven

"You're doing better, Bridgette. Isn't she Bart?"

Bart accompanied the two women to town after Jenks refused to ride in the rear rumble seat of Chloe's curricle. She made the choice of late to take the faster gig, rather than the farm wagon, to not lose more time away from the distillery. Precious time desperately needed to get her plant up and running a mere three weeks since the explosion.

As they approached the narrow bridge at Three Mile Creek, Bart hollered, "Pull left, pull left."

Bridgette failed to steer the horses toward the center of the bridge. The groom swung over her shoulders and yanked on the reins as a crackling gunshot pierced the air.

Bart slumped headlong between her and Bridgette.

"You're hurt," Bridgette screamed, dropping the leashes. His blood splattered her dress.

"Take the reins, Miss Tanner," Bart shouted as another shot rang forth, splintering the wood of a tulip poplar tree lining the road. "Make tracks, as fast as you can."

Chloe grabbed the slackened ribbons, pulling tight as the frightened horses leaped forward. She slapped the lines on the horses' backs, whipping them to a gallop, driving them across the bridge, scraping the glossy sides of her curricle as she drove through. A third shot sailed over their heads.

The two matched bays lathered at their mouths, as Chloe rode into the Tanner stableyard twenty minutes later, her carriage rocking to a halt. Her frantic shouts brought help. Jenks and a stableboy rushed from the stables and grabbed the panicked horses' bridles.

"Go get Milo," she ordered the youngster as she jumped down from the carriage. "Here, help me, Jenks. Now, Bridgette, push Bart off the seat so we can pull him down."

"I'm all right," Bart insisted, as he scooted from the back of the curricle holding his injured arm.

Jenks placed his arms under Bart's shoulder and assisted him to the tack room. Shoving a saddle off a wooden box, Chloe helped lower him, and leaned him against the wall. Blood trickled down his shirt sleeve dripping onto his pants and the ground. Bridgette tore his sleeve, pulling it away from the wound, while Chloe pumped water into a bucket at the farm sink.

"Jenks, tear me up a horse blanket, quick, I need to stop the bleeding."

"I'm okay," Bart said again his face losing all color.

"Here, let's get a compress on you." Chloe pressed the wool square against his upper arm.

"He's coming. Milo's on his way," the junior stable boy announced running in.

Milo tramped through the doorway. He gave one look at the scene in front of him before shoving Chloe away. "We've got a medicine kit, right above the sink, you idiots. What you trying to do? Give him blood poisoning."

Milo withdrew the blood-soaked cloth away from

Bart's arm. "One of you pull out that bottle of Number Five you've got hidden in these cabinets. Let's douse this...damn. Son of a biscuit, it is a bullet hole," he said surprised.

Bart slumped further against the wall. Bridgette held out the whiskey bottle. "No, give me some clean water and a cotton square to clean the wound." Milo swabbed the entry and exit points of the bullet shot, then fashioned a bandage from the aid kit around the groom's upper arm. "Bullet went straight through. You're one lucky man. Miss Bridgette, hold the bottle to his lips, if you can manage without slopping the contents all over him and give him a swallow."

With shaking hands, Bridgette did as she was told. After Milo tied off the bandage he rose and looked around him. "Someone mind telling me what the hell happened?"

"Some hunters must have been tracking game and didn't see us coming 'round the bend at the bridge," Chloe conveyed.

"Hell, 'scuse me, Miss Chloe, no one was hunting deer. They was shooting at us. Clear as day," Bart hissed.

"Shooting at you? Now, why would anybody want to shoot you?"

"Not me. He was aiming for the driver. Just so happen I was leaning over her when I took the bullet."

Bridgette collapsed in the chair by the desk.

"Not her," Bart murmured. "They were aiming at who they thought was driving."

All the men turned and looked at Chloe. Her broad-brimmed bonnet had slipped down on the perilous trip to the stable but was still tied around her neck.

Bridgette's navy denim bonnet, however, was still tied securely around her head, hiding her bright red tresses. She and Bridgette were similar in size. They looked the same from a distance. But a bullet was aimed at the driver, the owner of the conspicuous curricle.

Chloe felt the hair on her arms lift. She stood next to Milo gulping down a breath. Someone meant to shoot her? Her nerves, which up to this moment had not abandoned her, jumped. She exhaled then shook her limbs.

"Listen, everyone. We have enough rumors swirling about after the plant explosion. We don't need word to get out that we have someone shooting at us."

"I don't agree, Chloe. I think we need to report this to the sheriff."

"Milo, people are going to think we don't have things under control here. We're going to keep on working, stick to our regular responsibilities. We'll just be a little more vigilant."

"I don't like this. I don't like this one bit." Milo threw the extra bandage roll in a nearby bucket.

"We'll be on guard, more careful. But not one word of this gets out. Understood?" Five pairs of eyes stared back at her. Each nodded their tacit approval.

****

When Pen encountered Chloe's curricle at the blacksmith, he smiled. At long last, a chance to convince her in person that he did not have a hand in her plant's explosion. The mental image of her face when it was revealed he possessed dynamite he couldn't shake. Not one to waste time proclaiming innocence for something he did not do, he was eager, in Chloe's case, for her to know he was blameless. But she had purposely avoided him the past month.

He ran his hand across the curricle's scraped door, her plant foreman appeared from around the blacksmith's forge. The huge cylinder firepit bellowed and spewed as stall doors opened and closed.

"Ho, Milo. How's your two employees healing up?"

"You asking about the distillery workers?"

"Yeah."

"Virgil is going to be all right. He woke from his concussion as soon as they took him to his Ma's to nurse. Hector, not so good. Don't know if he'll ever get use of his hand again."

Pen stabbed the dirt surface with his boot toe. There was a tightening in his chest and limbs. "Milo, I didn't have anything to do with it."

"I figured you didn't, but I'm not the one you have to convince." He pinched his chin. "Which begs the question, if not you, who?"

Pen knitted his brows. "Yeah, that's the question for sure. Where is Miss Tanner?" he asked looking about. "She at the General store?"

"No, she's at her lawyer's office. I drove the curricle over here after dropping her off. Needed the blacksmith to look at the right wheel. Didn't like the look of it."

Pen picked up on Milo's tone. "What do you mean? Something she did driving, or are you thinking someone tampered with it?"

"Not sure, but the blacksmith said the damage looked like one of the spokes near been filed in two. Don't want to take no chance, after what happened last week."

"After what happened last week? Out with it, Milo," he demanded after sensing the foreman's reluctance.

"Well, won't hurt for you to know. Someone took a pot shot at Chloe's rig. Hit Bart who was riding jump seat, but we all think it was meant for Chloe."

A sudden burst from the giant forge flared up. The blacksmith's door swung shut. Pen's stomach lurched as he gasped for fresh air. He shuffled over to the heavy door and shoved it open. He stepped outside and leaned his back against the door and breathed in the fresh air. Paralyzed for a fleeting second, his heart raced. Milo followed him out.

"You all right?" he asked.

"Yeah, I'm fine. Bart okay?"

"Yeah, just a scratch."

"Damn, Milo. Where'd this happen?"

"Three Mile Creek."

"Why is she out gallivanting about the countryside after what happened to her factory?"

"Well, I guess you ain't heard. Not so many of them fancy city slicker lawyers and carpet bagging businessmen," he said as he spit sideways, "are excited about visiting a site which exploded and nearly killed two people. She's had to make runs to town a lot lately."

Pen looked at Milo, growing angrier by the minute. He muttered something to himself then looked up. "Well, I guess something will have to be done about that." And walked off.

****

Pen stretched his long legs out over the sidewalk after taking a seat on the bench outside Chloe's attorney's office door. Prepared to wait her out, he was surprised when she exited within minutes of him taking a seat.

"Mr. Kittrell?" A brief look of surprise was replaced with a pained expression.

"Chloe." He had forgotten how dark her green eyes could turn. How, when she wrinkled her nose and winced, her face was still beautiful to him. "I sent you a note. I wanted to see you."

"I know."

He stood in front of her. "Can we walk for a minute?" he asked offering his arm. She clutched her briefcase to her body, refusing to touch him.

"Milo is waiting for me at the blacksmith's if you want to walk in that direction." She turned and sped with quick steps toward the blacksmith's.

Undeterred, he kept step with her. "My intent was to tell you in person, I had nothing to do with your plant's explosion. I reported to the sheriff I had dynamite stolen from my plant. But there is no evidence who took the sticks or even if the two events are connected."

"Really?" She raised one arched brow. "And you expect me to believe that?"

"No." He fisted his hands in frustration. His face darkening as they walked along. "I'll find out who did this. In the meantime, you need to be careful."

"Mr. Kittrell, I have a distillery to run."

"I sent help. You didn't have to turn it down."

"I don't want your handouts." She turned away after biting her lip.

"I'm not the enemy here and turning down an honest offer to help is just plain stupid." He reached out, touching her fingers holding her briefcase. His chest tightened as she pushed him away, recoiling from the insensitive remark. His anger toward her at this moment for not accepting his help and believing in his innocence drove away any effort to convince her in a different manner. *Damn, she is one stubborn woman.*

"I hope you do discover who did do the damage to my distillery. But I'd advise you to not spend too much time demonizing those temperance people who seem to sing psalms and read Bible passages. Perhaps you should spend more time looking closer to home. Good day, Mr. Kittrell." She nodded. "I see my carriage is ready."

****

Pen detected the familiar whippoorwill cry as soon as he turned off the beaten mountain path and took the trail up to Eagle Point. By the second turkey call, he knew he was being watched and his location pinpointed. He guided Patience gingerly over the deadwood and fallen leaves, staying clear of the embedded rocks, taking no chance of a copperhead striking his mare's legs. It had been a couple of years since he'd been this far north, the summer foliage made it more difficult to follow a path, but he knew the area well from quail hunting. And all you had to do was follow the smell, even if you couldn't spot the tell-tale smoke from the illegal still.

"Come on, girl, we're almost there," he said, transitioning from a walk to a trot as he reached the bald clearing.

"Been a while." The county's oldest moonshiner greeted Pen. His observant, beady eyes ran up and down Pen's frame when he dismounted, then took in his gray mare, nodding in approval at the horse. The ancient maverick had been hunched over his shack's porch rail as if waiting for him. Pen's mouth twitched, recalling just who'd sent that fateful batch of moonshine over to the Tanners' as a bereavement offering the night of the funeral. The turn of events that completely tossed his life upside down from that day forward.

One of his henchmen took Patience's reins as Pen walked toward the ramshackle structure. "Nice piece of horseflesh you have there." The moonshiner eyed his mare before turning to Pen. "You don't favor your pa so much—favor your ma more. Only had one flaw, your ma—married the wrong man."

"Not here to discuss my family tree, Homer." Pen had always maintained awe for the man who was a living legend. He stood tall even with his stooped back, and his salt and pepper beard had to be one for the record books. For whatever reason, maybe it was an independent streak, or the absolute detest of giving a nickel to the government, but where Kittrell and Tanner went legit some years ago, Homer Burns remained content brewing his illegal mash.

"Well, your pa stole my best whiskey recipe, so I don't know what else you could want from me," he said as he spit tobacco juice to the side. The giant bloodhound at his feet scampered off the porch to give the visitor a friendlier greeting.

"I know you have men coming here looking for work who can't get hired elsewhere—most likely 'cause of something in their past. I need you to find me a bodyguard," he asked while leaning down to pet the dog.

"Why you need a bodyguard? I knows you got enough Injun blood in you not to let a fellow slip up on you, and I heard tell you won the sharpshooting medal at that fancy school they sent you to."

"Not for me, it's for a lady."

Homer stood straight, intrigued. "Sounds interesting."

"Need one for Miss Chloe Tanner."

"The pretty Boss Lady?"

"Yes." Pen rubbed his mustache. "She doesn't have any help except for a lame foreman, couple of stable hands, two pencil pushers, and a new general manager so raw I wouldn't trust more than a rattlesnake shedding his skin."

"Consider it done," the ancient moonshiner pronounced, tugging at his scraggly beard, narrowing his red-rimmed eyes. "Don't think I don't know who's kept the revenuers out of this part of the county for a bit. I owe you. I'll send you someone next week."

Pen left with a slight peace of mind. He ran his hand through his hair before replacing his hat. After mounting his gray mare, he patted her on the neck. "Let's head home, girl." Nudging her about, he headed down the steep mountain trail.

Why, oh why, does this have to happen to me now? The explosion at Chloe's plant was enough to cause him to lose sleep at night, but when Milo told him someone had taken shots at her carriage it made his blood run cold. It was akin to splashing into an icy lake in the middle of the winter, waking him up from some deep sleep-walking slumber.

Chloe meant more to him than a beautiful face and an alluring body. He closed his eyes. He wanted her. He wanted her so he could breathe. So he could enjoy life, commit to her, marry her if she would have him.

An electric jolt hit him. He had fallen in love. A love so deep, even if he could not have her for his own, he still wished for her to be safe, happy. But that wasn't enough. *Damn*. He wanted her for himself. Just had to figure a way to win her heart.

Chapter Twelve

"Milo, why do you think I need a bodyguard?" Chloe was incensed when introduced to Will Irwin. "Mr. Irwin, would you mind waiting outside my office door a minute."

She turned on Milo as soon as the door closed. "Well?"

"Chloe, we can't lose any more workers to gunshots and explosions. You've not done a darn thing different since we had all these dad-blamed happenings over the past month. When Will is not driving you to town, he can help patrol the premises."

"My word, Milo. Did you even get a good look at that man? More likely he'll be hauling off the distillery's safe while we're asleep in our beds." She slammed her hands on her hips. As formidable as the man looked, judging by the jagged scar running from his temple to his chin and a number of missing teeth, he was not always the winner of previous fights.

"This is not an argument you're going to win. I'm your foreman, and my responsibility is to take care of the plant property and grounds, anything valuable. And with that business taking place at the top of the 'Y' of the Wishbone, we can't be too careful."

"Have you been talking to Pen Kittrell? I don't trust him. You know I don't. There's nothing going on up there but a couple of locals trying to build a bridge."

"Don't think that's all it is," he scoffed.

"All right you win. Tell my minder I have to go to town after lunch. He can drive me in the barouche."

It was two hours after lunch by the time Chloe walked out of the house carrying her red leather briefcase and usual stack of papers stuffed inside. "Will, can you take me to Deane's Law Office, it's next door to the courthouse."

"Yes, ma'am," the mammoth man answered as he assisted her into the coach.

"I've left the top down, Miss Tanner. Might be a smart thing for people to see you got a new driver."

"Very thoughtful," she admitted staring at his solid back.

After they crossed Three Mile Bridge, Chloe opened up a conversation. There wasn't any way she was going to ride for an hour and not speak to her driver. "Will, what do you know about a bridge they're building at the top of the Y?"

"I know they's using parole convicts for the labor. That should tell you a lot," he said spitting out tobacco juice on his side of the coach.

"What do you mean?"

"If you saw people's faces as the state militia marched prisoners into coal mining towns to take the places of the husbands, fathers, and brothers of men who put food on their tables, you'd know what I mean. Anybody who'd use convict labor instead of paying a man a fair wage for a living is the true criminal in my book." He snapped the reins hard.

Chloe grabbed the sides of the coach. She held on tight to the hand rungs. *Merciful heavens*. A definite sore point. Did she need a bodyguard from her bodyguard?

When they reached Deane's law office, her attorney stood waiting for her on the steps to his office. His usual lighthearted demeanor was replaced by apprehension.

"Come on inside, Miss Tanner," he said helping her from of her carriage.

Once in his office, he got right to the point. "How much corn reserves have you got at your north county silo?"

Nervousness gripped her insides. "Why do you ask?"

"A telegram came through an hour ago. There's been a wildfire on the Sawyer property. I made a telephone call to a fellow attorney over there. He said they been fighting it two days."

"A fire in the fields? How? We haven't seen any lightning this whole summer. Please tell me it was an accident."

"Not according to my friend. Says evidence looks like the fire was set on purpose. Witnesses saw some transients camping on what they thought was an unusual place to start a campfire. Too late to do anything about it by the time it was reported. The farmers are just trying to control any more startups for now."

"You know I'm their exclusive buyer for their yields." Chloe collapsed in her attorney's office chair and leaned back trying to relieve the caved-in pressure in her chest. Her stomach rolled waiting for Deane's answer.

"Yes. I know."

"Any other fires reported? For instance, on the

west side of the Wishbone? Near Kittrell's?"

"Hadn't heard of any."

****

Calm down. She scolded herself stomping away from her lawyer's office. *This was probably one big coincidence. Fires happen all the time.* Drifters wandered throughout the county, setting up temporary camps wherever they liked. Not giving a darn what happened once they left—skedaddling like cockroaches into the night. It was impossible not to worry until she calculated the distillery's corn reserves. The Sawyers had two giant silos but were they full? She wished she could collapse on the return trip home and roll up into a ball. But she refused to crumble and did her best to shake off the imaginings that this latest setback was not an accident.

Both Milo and McCoy were waiting for her at her home's front door when Will drove up the drive. The looks on their faces told her they had heard the news too.

"Fire is bad stuff." Corbin shook his head. "Won't know how bad until we check our inventory. Might as well hear the other bad news," he relayed as they trudged down to the distillery. "When I called the bottling company in Cincinnati this morning to place an order, they said there was a six-month's backorder on the bottling machines. And you want to know who bought their last three?"

She lifted her shoulders, dreading what he would say next. "Go ahead, tell me."

"Pen Kittrell."

I hate him. I hate him. Oh, why did I ever trust that man for one minute. She swallowed hard, ducking her head as if taking a blow. Today's twin pieces of news could not hit her any harder. She hurt. Her lungs constricted with each breath she took. Why were her cornfields the only ones burned? And Pen Kittrell purchasing the last of the bottling machines.

Was this another attempt by Pen to get her to cave? Could he in fact be behind all her troubles? Those machines, they had to set him back a pretty penny. Did he have a backer somewhere? Someone underwriting the whole lot in order to take over her company?

I'll get him back. Somehow. Someway. I'll think of a plan.

****

Chloe woke from a recurring dream. Lips pressing kisses on every inch of her flesh. Kisses like whiskey, touching every nerve in her body. A husky voice whispering words of love in her ear. Tossing from side to side, she touched her heart where a yearning ache had settled, then brought her fingers to her lips. She sat straight up in bed, drawing her knees up to her chest as if protecting herself from another onslaught. She rubbed her arms, repressing the vivid memory she awoke from.

The tug-of-war with her brain over her feelings for Pen Kittrell was more than an ongoing nuisance. Oh, how she wished her attraction to him would go away. Had she ever been so miserable in all her life? Was there any release from her conflicting emotions? Could happiness be found with a man who wanted power over the very thing that mattered most to her? Did she think she could lie with another man after being with Pen? She must be insane. All the more reason she was convinced she could never marry. Should she just give in? Form a perfectly scandalous affair and the devil take the hindmost?

No. Nothing so good for that man. I'll figure a way. A way to get some revenge. He needs rye to make his special whiskey. And Kittrell's believes rye whiskey produced over the winter tastes smoother. Yes, he'll need new rye. Yes, he will. And lots of it.

****

The Tri-County Auction House was packed to the rafters. Farmers, merchants, grain buyers, and onlookers from around a one-hundred-fifty-mile radius filled the giant weather-beaten wood converted warehouse. After this summer's drought, next year's grain reserves would be slim pickings. Attendance at the auction was at an all-time high. Corbin McCoy accompanied Chloe on the trip, along with her driver and groom. Milo had refused to attend the sale once she made her plans known to her foreman. Too old, he said, to be limping about a bunch of people who hung 'round auctions for the free food and swigs of moonshine snuck between the parked wagons. In reality, she knew he objected to her attending. It had been less than a week after the reported wildfires and much too soon to be spending precious capital on grain when facing unpredictable times.

After she signed for their bid paddles, Corbin accompanied her, meandering between the rows of barrels, checking the different varieties of grain. Each barrel represented a yield for sale and was marked with a number and the name of the grower. Knowing the farmer who cultivated the grains was critical because inspecting wheat and rye were more difficult, unlike corn where the stalks and kernels could be examined. Will and Bart, content to watch her and the populace inspect the different varieties of grain, took seats in the top of the wooden bleachers. It was from this vantage point, seated between her driver and general manager that Chloe joined them, barely settled before she saw Pen walk in.

The usual crowd of hangers-on hovered around his over six-foot frame. Men patted him on the back, a few women swayed enticingly into his sphere. She knew he sensed her, even when he glanced around the room nonchalantly. No surprise registered in his eyes when he found her. Merciful heavens, he gave no acknowledgment, deciding not to draw attention by recognizing her in public at such a distance.

Protected on both sides by her employees, Pen dare not try to sit with her. Besides, he'll be too curious and want to watch and see what brought her to the auction. He took a seat on the same level on the opposite set of bleachers. She smoothed the skirt of her fetching seagreen silk dress and waited for the bidding to begin.

"Ladies and gentlemen, each and every one of you have been apprised of today's rules. Forty-percent down today followed by balance in sixty days," the auction's Colonel instructed. "Each participant must be registered and have their paddle in their possession during the entire proceedings to be returned at end of today's sale. We will move from left to right. Corn, wheat, then rye. All sold by the bushel, not by the pound folks. This ain't a tobacco sale. We'll begin with batch number one, corn from the Carson farm.

"Are you ready?" shouted the Colonel. A brass bell clanged signaling the start of the auction. "Oh, Ye. Oh, Ye. And what am I bid for it? And what am I give for it? Say now…any buddy wanna bid? Any buddy want to buy 'em? Would ya bid? Would ya bid? Would ya buy em? Would ya buy 'em? Now at eighty-three, eighty-three? Who'll give me eighty-three, yep, eighty-four, hey bidder now, hey bid a bit, yep, eighty-five..." The auctioneer raced through the corn, yield after yield, knocking down the lots cents below high estimates.

"To the rye, we shall go. To the rye, we shall go," the auctioneer sang out after the successful conclusion of the wheat auction. "Folks we just have two batches, but prime grain they are. From local farms, the Cloverbend and Wild Root, long-time growers in these here parts. This is the last auction of the summer for rye. No more in the state. For the Cloverbend batch, who'll give me a dollar ten, now a dollar ten?"

Chloe raised her paddle.

"To the pretty lady in the top row, who will give me a dollar fifteen, yep, to the gentleman sitting high on the other side. Folks, fine rye this is, who will give me a dollar twenty? Yes, back to the little lady. Who will give me dollar-twenty-five? Yeah, to the gentleman. One dollar thirty?"

Chloe raised her paddle again.

"Yes, says the lovely lady. One dollar thirty-five, one dollar thirty-five anyone? Sir?"

"Going once, going twice, going three times. Sold it. Sold it. Sold it. Folks say hello to a good buy. Sold to the very lovely lady." The gavel hammered the block on the podium with a sound thump.

Chloe nodded her head to the auctioneer's salute.

"Folks this remaining batch may be the final bushels for a while. Listen to what I say—the last of the year," the auctioneer pitched. "Farmers tell me without any rain this summer—this yield might be the whole shebang for a spell. Let that digest in your gut a moment.

"Good people, let's start the bidding where we left off. Who'll give me a dollar thirty-five? Yes, to the gentleman on the first row. Yep, one-forty, yeah, to lucky number thirteen sitting right in front of me. One-fifty, yeah, one-sixty, yes, one-seventy-five?" There was a pause. The lucky number thirteen put his paddle away. "Folks this will be the last offering of rye grain until Christmas. That is, if farmers can get rye to seed in the hard-packed ground this fall. I'm up here on the mountain, got to bid it, to make it. Yep, to the gentleman in the top rafter."

Pen had bid the highest anyone could remember for local rye. But the auctioneer sensing a rivalry stuck with his proven tactics and chants. "The hammer's high, I got to fly." He shot a look to the left of Pen pretending to see another bidder. "Who'll give me one-eighty?"

Chloe raised her paddle and held it in the air longer than usual. Corbin pulled at her hand. "We don't need any more rye Miss Tanner. This is a bigger batch. We can't afford the down payment on this price alone."

"Stop," she whispered. "I know what I'm doing." Corbin stood and stepped away.

"Who will give me two dollars?" The auctioneer jumped his price knowing he had a buyer, just not sure which one.

Pen raised his paddle.

"We're at two dollars, two dollars a bushel, two-ten anyone?" Chloe sat, motionless.

"Two dollars is the bid, anyone? Going, going…"

"Two-twenty-five," called out Chloe. A suspended

awe arose from the crowd.

"Two-thirty, a bushel," the auctioneer called, unwilling to stop. "Don't look at her, you got the money," he badgered. Chloe kept her paddle aloft. She held the last bid. Without blinking she stared across at Pen. The entire arena hushed in anticipation. "Sir? Going once, going twice?"

"Two-thirty," Pen shouted. A collective gasp escaped from the onlookers.

"We're at two-thirty folks. Do I have a higher bid? A raise from Miss Pretty Lady?"

Chloe sat back, wishing she could see Pen squirm. Smiling at the auctioneer, she gave a too rich for me dismissal sign and slowly lowered her paddle. She was bowing out.

"Going once, going twice, sold to the gentleman in the back, for two-thirty a bushel," the auctioneer barked slamming his gavel down. "Folks, I believe this is a state record price."

A quick calculation in her head, she figured Pen was going to have to cough up two thousand dollars for the down payment alone. *Hope that sticks to his craw.* She smiled to herself, then glanced over at Pen. Staring at her with an amused gleam, he gave a tip of his favorite hat. He knew exactly what she had pulled off.

Corbin returned to her side and took a cleansing breath. "Miss Chloe, all I could think of while you were bidding was where were we going to put that grain. And the auctioneer? What would he have done once you told him you had no way to pay the bid?"

"He'd gone to the next highest bidder and offered the sale to him. You shouldn't have worried. You know I didn't need that much rye. I just wanted Mr. Kittrell to have to see what it was like to have to dig deep into his pockets." Once Milo heard what she had done, he would say she'd won a small skirmish in a big battle, but it sure did make her feel a whole lot better.

As they approached the closing table, she felt a touch at her elbow. Aware it was Pen, she turned tilting her head and giving her most disarming smile.

"Congratulations. I think you won on both bids, in my book anyway," he confessed.

"Did you forget, Mr. Kittrell?" She hoped her green eyes sparkled. "I told you once I learned how to play poker. I knew I had nothing in my hand. But the trick is, isn't it, not to let the other players know. Have a pleasant rest of your day."

Chapter Thirteen

Three days after the auction, Pen observed Chloe ride into town with her new driver. An earlier visit to the exchange hall alerted him of a three o'clock visit she would be making to her attorney's office. He ran his hand through his hair. Damn, she was becoming ever more difficult. It should have been no surprise, her duping him at the auction. Guess she wasn't happy about him ordering the bottling machines. Payback she'd say.

His initial reluctant admiration for her turned to full-fledge respect. She ran her distillery under harsh scrutiny, from her employees to the townsfolk to her peers. Adverse conditions men were not subject to. He, among others, had underestimated her. Her character allowed her to survive as a southerner within those northeastern cliques she was raised in, then she came down here and prevailed as a woman running a male business, quite successfully, he had to acknowledge.

He knew something about being an outsider. You had to grow thick skin. His identical school uniform didn't distinguish him from his well-heeled classmates. But sisters and cousins attending cotillions and other functions were steered clear of the cadet with medals on his chest, for fear of them setting up more than a flirtation with the heir to a whiskey distillery.

"Good afternoon, Miss Tanner." Pen raised his hat

as she exited from Deane's law office a half hour later. "If you are walking to the courthouse, may I please show you something I have upstairs in the room adjoining the exchange hall?"

She frowned toward her driver who was sitting on the coach seat eating a bag of peanuts, so engrossed he seemed to not notice who was accosting her on the sidewalk. She sniffed before speaking. "Mr. Kittrell, it just so happens I am going the same way, but I'm very short on time."

After giving a slight bow, he let her take the lead down the narrow walkway. As he followed her, he wondered how long she would keep up the act of snubbing him. Surely, she did not still believe he was the one who blasted the front end of her factory to shreds? Or burned her cornfields? More likely, she was infuriated about the bottling machines.

"Chloe, whatever you think of me, I would never destroy property or hurt anyone to get ahead in business. Can we get that straight between us?"

"Or purchase the remaining bottling machines available for almost a year?"

"Ah, you're sore about that." He grinned relieved.

"Yes, as a matter of fact, I am. Since I occupy a distillery with the only other bottling machine in the state. A machine which happens to need repair because someone stole or lost the very dynamite which blew up my distillery. Which doesn't matter in the end, because I perchance won't have enough corn to make product because someone 'accidentally' burned all my fields."

Pen stopped, the hurt in her face was palpable. "Please, come with me."

He guided her inside and up the back staircase of

the courthouse. He showed her into a small office in the back of the exchange room's atrium hall. Clearly a man's province, as demonstrated by the artwork of scantily clothed women hung on every wall.

"That day we were out riding together at the top of the Wishbone," he said as they entered. "Do you recall me asking Jenks if he'd seen anything like the tethered pile of timbers we saw on the east side?"

"Jenks told me you thought someone was trying to build a bridge."

"It's not a bridge, come look at these." Pen pointed to the table with hand drawn ink sketches illustrating what appeared to be some kind of an overpass.

"What is this?"

"It's a dam."

Chloe leaned in to study the sketches Pen held. She smelled so wonderful, like the first days of summer. Honeysuckle and strawberries. Did she know what she did to him when she stood this close? "Look at this one here. You can see no water coming underneath."

Chloe squinted hard, trying to make out the specifics of what he was talking about.

"Here." Pen handed her a pair of bifocals he picked up from a small desk in the corner. "They're my accountant's, he wouldn't mind."

She studied the glasses, looking them over a second, before placing them on the ridge of her nose.

"It's nice to know you aren't perfect," he said.

A wry smile edged her lips.

"You should have told me to bring my attorney here too."

"Speaking of your attorney, you aren't selling more than fifty-one percent of your company to anyone to raise capital, are you?"

"Why is that any of your business? Are you thinking of buying my stock?"

"Might be. But the crucial reason is—if you sell out—I'd like to know who I should contact to help me fight this."

"Fight what?"

"If it's a dam, and I'm positive it is, someone's building it to control the water."

Her eyes widened at the revelation. She took off the bifocals and rubbed her eyes, then placed them on again to look at the drawings.

"I didn't know the land above the Wishbone was titled," he added. "And neither one of our families are on those deeds."

"You seem to know a lot about this."

"Damn right," he said watching her wince. "But there's a lot I don't know."

"It appears most of the construction is on my side of the Wishbone. A lot seems to be happening only to me, Pen. Perhaps, you do not need to worry so much," she suggested as she pushed the pictures aside.

"Don't kid yourself, we have to stick together. Whoever this is, is not just after one of us. And corn, rye, bottling machines are nothing if we don't have water."

"Who's behind this?"

Pen hesitated a moment. "So far, I haven't been able to find out. But an outfit called the Clearmont Management Company hired state convicts for the labor up there. The construction appears like they're building a dam for sure. I wanted to show you this evidence first. As long as you are running your company, you're the one who will have to make the hard decisions."

"Hard decisions, like what?"

"You'll know soon enough, I'm sure."

"Well, I better be going. My driver will be coming to look for me soon if I don't appear."

"Oh, I don't think…you're right. I'll escort you to your carriage."

She passed the glasses back to him. "No need, but thank you." When their fingers touched, she jerked her hand back from his like it had been burned by a hot coal.

"Chloe?"

"Pen." She shook her head and looked down. "I have to go." She turned with a quick swish of her skirts and was out the door.

****

"Miss Tanner." Her driver met her at the door outside the courthouse.

"Sorry I took so long, Will. I'm ready to go now."

"Well, as to that, Miss, there's two gentlemen," he paused to spit tobacco juice in the street, "wanting to see you. I came to fetch you. Seems as if they are hanging about in your lawyer's office right now."

"Can I help you?" Chloe asked, entering her attorney's office. Two men dressed in rumpled slick suits stood waiting for her. *Revenuers*. Where was her attorney when she needed him?

"Miss Tanner?" asked the tall man with a heavily pomaded head and bowler hat which he did not remove until she entered. "We're from the Treasury Department for the State. We have come from Nashville to conduct an audit of your whiskey inventory against our records for tax purposes," he said hooking his thumbs into his belt loops and thrusting his pelvis forward.

"Where's my attorney?" She glanced about the room again.

" 'Spec he's gone looking for you."

Chloe held down the bile rising in her throat before answering the man as he flashed an identification card. "Unbeknownst apparently to you in Nashville, I have suffered an inexplicable explosion and fire that took the roof off my distillery, including my offices. Paperwork is everywhere. I don't have time for this."

The other man, who had watched her with beady eyes, stepped in front of her face. "Fire. Where have I heard that before, Dwayne? Most common excuse we hear for skipping out on taxes, I'd say. Seems like you could come up with a better excuse than them bourbon makers used in Kentucky."

"Just what are you accusing me of? And who sent you? Are you by chance spot checking, excuse me, auditing, other distilleries in the vicinity? Like Kittrell's for example?"

"No. Don't recall we have any concerns there."

"Bet not."

"We calculated this number of barrels based on two warehouses." The man with the pomade head thrust a file in front of her.

Chloe shoved the record backward. "You know we don't pay taxes on whiskey barrels until they are three years old."

The taller man's eyes flickered. "Seems like our little lady does know her way around whiskey. We had heard that. Just a forewarn, ma'am, we will be back. Thursday week. Be seeing you." He replaced his bowler and the pair left without further ceremony.

"Oh, Mother of Pearl," Chloe swore out loud. She counted to twenty, then hoisted up her skirt and headed out the door. Not caring who she shocked on the sidewalk by revealing ten inches of petticoats and a pair of purple silk stockings, she flew to the courthouse. This time she raced up the front stairs, stopping on the second-floor ledge which gave her a full view of the giant elevated exchange boards and the small group observing workers scribble in the latest spirit prices. Pen Kittrell had commandeered a leather chair and laid his head back with his feet propped on a nearby ottoman watching the men chalk up the numbers while sipping whiskey from a cut-glass tumbler.

"Mr. Kittrell."

Surprised in mid sip, when he heard her voice, Pen spilled remnants of his drink down his chin and onto his shirt. He wiped his mouth as he rose to greet her. "Miss Tanner."

"I need to speak to you privately."

"Certainly."

Calmly, he motioned for her to come toward his back office. She hoped he sensed her fury.

"You don't need to shut the door," she said.

"I think I better." Detecting her anger, he turned and closed his door behind her. "What's this? What's upset you all of a sudden?" he asked in his smooth unhurried manner.

"Don't act surprised. I doubt very seriously you didn't know two revenuers from the tax office were waiting to confront me at my attorney's office just now. You know their every movement."

"No, I didn't, believe you me, I would never call

revenuers down here for any reason," he said leaning into her.

"Have you been drinking *my* whiskey?" The irrational thought came to her head as soon as she detected the distinctive brown sugar and caramel scent with a touch of vanilla. Her scent, her signature scent all over him. She inched toward the door, but his powerful body blocked the way out.

He smiled. "And if I was, what of it?"

"If you were, that's the closest you'll ever get to me again." He stood close, staring at her enraged face. He reached out his hand to draw hers into his. She wrenched back her hand. "I can't prove you called them, but those men from Nashville are coming back next week. And I can't prove you had anything to do with half destroying my distillery either, or burning my cornfields, but don't think I don't know you are checking my whiskey stock prices each week. I know that for certain. I'm leaving now," she hissed. "But not before warning you to leave Tom Tanner Tennessee Whiskey alone. And don't bother to follow me. I have a bodyguard now, who would beat you within an inch if I asked him to."

With this last declaration, she was gone.

****

Pen returned back to his seat by the exchange boards and retrieved his tumbler lifting it in a salute to the direction Chloe had exited. *I wish you were the whiskey*. He downed what was left of the amber liquid, wrapping his tongue in the flavorful and delicious caramel. The finish a long and lingering one.

****

She was so consumed in her anger she almost

jumped in her carriage for Will to take her home. For once thankful for a non-talkative driver, Chloe seethed in her self-righteousness the entire way back to Tanner Place. *I've had just about enough of that man's interference, if not outright infringement.* The meddling, the incursion, the invasion of her business dealings, how deep did it go? How involved was Pen? Was he just waiting in the wings ready to snap up her company or reap the benefits from helping someone else in a takeover? Who else could be behind the mounting misfortunes attempting to topple her precarious hold of Tom Tanner's Tennessee Whiskey?

If Clearmont Management Company was behind the threats and intimidations and were the ones who called the revenuers, not Pen, like he insisted, it put him in a different light. Could she ever trust him, though? Did it matter? Liars and cheats. Sometimes you can't help who your heart falls for, you just have to deal with it. *Somehow.*

What Pen divulged regarding Clearmont put Jed Sanders, the other person she suspected was behind her troubles, in a different light. From what she knew of Sanders, he seemed like the type of man who'd cut his losses and run. When he worked for her grandfather, had Sanders' sole interest been in lining his pockets while no one watched? Were her mother's feelings for him true?

When Chloe arrived home, she sought out her mother. She searched through the house before locating her in the backyard garden. A little boy traipsed after her, carrying a straw basket. Her mother would pick a vegetable and, after saying something to him, he would nod his head and hold out the basket. As she neared them, she heard his young voice chattering to her.

"Mother?" She glanced at her mother then down at the little boy, it was Raelynn's son.

"Chloe, I believe you've met Dillon. He's been helping me pick strawberries and tomatoes."

"I see. How are you doing, young man?"

"Well, Miss."

"Dillon, take this basket to your mother. Tell her she can have this batch of strawberries if she'll send you back tomorrow to help fill another basket for me."

He sent a dimpled smile to both ladies before turning to run down the hill.

"I didn't know you knew Dillon, Mother. Do you know who his father is?"

"I don't believe it's my business to ask."

"It might be." She tilted her head. "Mother, you have to have guessed."

"I have. And, oh Chloe, I'm so happy, yet I don't want Raelynn to take him away, so I haven't said anything to her."

"Mother, we will work this out. The child's a blessing to us all." Her heart swelled with happiness for her mother. *Finally, something to be happy about.*

"Where have you been?" her mother asked changing the subject.

"I've been in town. And besides being confronted by state tax revenuers, I just found out there is an outfit called the Clearmont Management Company building what appears to be a dam up on the Wishbone before it splits. I think it is another attempt to have me give up, to sell out. If that's so, I fear I was wrong in suspecting Jed Sanders of being involved in our distillery's explosion. I'm telling you this because if you truly care for Mr. Sanders, I won't stand in your way. We never did bring charges against him for trying to steal from us, so there's no encumbrance."

Her mother stood and brushed her skirts. "Thank you, Chloe, for sharing this with me. No, I don't have feelings for Mr. Sanders. Not now, anyway. In fact, I have been wanting to tell you I have been corresponding with a longtime acquaintance of mine."

"Oh, someone I know?"

"Much too soon…"

Chloe looked at her mother's face and could swear she was blushing. In fact, the more she studied her, the more changes she observed. Her restored interest in gardening had brought color to her whole face, not merely her cheeks. And the dark circles under her eyes had all but disappeared. She should have noticed yesterday when she woke and found her mother already in the kitchen supervising jam making with their cook. So surprised to discover her mother up before dawn, she failed to observe any transformations in her mother's appearance.

"I'm here, when you're ready to talk." Chloe reached out and patted her mother's arm. "There's someone else I hope I'm wrong about."

"Yes?"

"I'm just not sure yet. There's a lot I don't know."

Chapter Fourteen

"Those two fellows Will Irwin picked up in Miss Chloe's wagon wouldn't be the same revenuers from Nashville who were here last week?" Pen questioned Chloe's attorney with a broad smile as he crossed over from the courthouse to join him outside his law office. Smoke billowed from the train engine as the locomotive departed the station.

"I do believe they are," Wendell Deane answered as he stepped out of the way of a young matron carrying a baby and pulling her toddler's arm behind her. "That's one thing you can always count on in regard to government workers, they're consistent. They said they'd be back in one week to investigate Tanner's. And here they are." Both men laughed whole-heartedly. "What time are we supposed to meet at the Hatchie Camp whistle-stop?" Deane asked.

Pen looked at his pocket watch. "It's early yet. I'd say the four o'clock meet up would be about right." He rubbed the back of his neck, then fisted his hand, and punched the porch pillar as he watched Chloe's driver head out of town.

****

Three hours later, Pen reined in Patience, slid off his horse, and tied her to a rotted post. He reached the out-of-way wood framed church by taking a short cut over a dry creek bed. The few low hanging clouds still showed no promise of rain as he glanced up at the empty bell turret in the crumbling steeple. The remote location served as the ideal meeting spot, with its proximity to the whistle-stop for mail drops and pickups on their way to Nashville.

The front door scuffed the threshold as he pushed it open. A couple of starlings fluttered up to the rafters as he entered the musty, empty structure. He removed his hat, swatting away cobwebs before taking a seat in the back. The whitewashed, stained walls stood in contrast to the dark plank floors and rickety wood pews. Sunlight made its utmost effort to filter in through pollen and dirt-crusted windows. A driftwood cross hung above a solitary pulpit.

Creaking wagon wheels sounded from outside. Muffled voices were heard over horses whinnying from the same direction. The parson's side door behind the pulpit scratched open. Two men, their heads covered with hoods and their hands tied behind their backs, marched in.

"Ten more steps, then stop," Will Irwin commanded, coming in behind them. "There's a bench to your left, when you feel it with your legs, take a seat." Using the shotgun barrel, Chloe Tanner's massive driver prodded them forward.

He pressed the long gun across the first man's shoulder, pushing him onto the first-row pew. The second man jerked back when poked. He stumbled forward and kicked a wooden crate placed in front of the pews. From the back of the church, Pen heard the unmistakable rattling sounds coming from the disturbed box.

"For God's sake, brother. Have mercy," the

frightened man pleaded, hobbling back.

"I said, sit down now." Chloe's driver pulled the man by his jacket before shoving him to the pew.

Stump, scrape, stump scrape. Another discernable sound emanated from the other side of the same door the men had entered.

"Whoa, whoa there, don't need to be so unsettled," a raspy voice soothed. Homer Burns, the ancient moonshiner, emerged, leaning on his hand-hewn walking stick. He climbed the altar steps, dragging his right foot behind him. The old miscreant reached the pulpit area, then turned around smoothing his long gray beard before signaling to Will.

He removed the men's hoods. Daring not to budge, the men stared motionless at the figure before them.

"You old buzzard, whoever you are, release us right now. You have no right to hold us," the man who had struggled earlier spat out. "We represent the state of Tennessee, and you'll be in a heap of trouble if you don't let us go immediately."

Homer pounded his cane, with a gnarled grasp, on the wood floor. The other man flinched, reflexively kicking the box before him. Rattling echoed through the deserted place of worship. He slunk back into the pew corner, darting his gaze between the man at the pulpit and the container before him.

"Shush now," Homer commanded. "These here snakes are used to Sunday services. They're cranky for sure being toted out on a Thursday. Now let me see. Why are we here? Yes, I remember now. I brung you two fine gentlemen into church today to have what we call a 'Come to Jesus' moment," he orated in a sing-song manner. "We here in these parts are Godfearing men. And we don't hold with anyone threatening our womenfolk. And a little birdie told me that's what you done. Some say a serpent won't strike an innocent man. Want to give the theory a test?"

"No, no. For pity's sake, brother."

"I recall a boarding house in Nashville on Charlotte Avenue. I'd pass it on the way to visit a friend in Bucksnort, used to house government workers. You wouldn't by chance be a resident there, either of you two gentlemen?"

Neither man uttered a word. "One thing I can tell you"—the old moonshiner spoke with relish—"city snakes are meaner than country snakes. They will find you and seek out those who tell falsehoods. Might not kill you, but you'd be sure to lose a limb if they bit you. Once knowed a man who cut off his own arm to stop the venom from doing worse. So, I heartily recommend you hightail it back to where you came from and leave us country folk alone for good.

"Reckon I shouldn't have to ask for your word in a house of worship, but I believe I will, unless you want to take one of our country snakes with you as a reminder of your promise?"

"No brother, no way in hell I'd ever come out here again—wherever this Godforsaken place is."

"Me neither, I swear on my mother's grave."

"Well, ain't that solemn." Homer pursed his lips giving each man a glassy stare before motioning for Will to come forward and replace their hoods.

"Guess we got just enough time to get these fine gentlemen to the whistle-stop for the mail pick up this afternoon."

****

Hells, bells. Who would ever think the old reprobate had a romantic bone in his body? Pen rose from the back pew and saluted the old scoundrel with a tip of his hat. When a plan was being hatched to get rid of the irksome revenuers, Pen was surprised when Will announced Homer Burn's offer to help. The gesture had to be motivated by more than a deep-seated hatred of all things governmental. Apparently, the attractive new female distillery owner had an admirer from afar.

Pen sighed. He wished he could do more to help Chloe. Until he could get to the bottom of who was behind the unscrupulous and ruthless destruction happening to Tanner Whiskey, they had to play their cards close to their vests. He looked forward to one day sharing with Chloe today's escapade. He'd love to see those green eyes dance in glee. He shook his head. *City snakes. Really!*

He ambled forward to assist Will. Chloe's attorney would be waiting at the whistle-stop with an official mail pouch, cumbersome enough for the train to stop long enough for him and Will to toss a couple of extra bags in the mail car. *Yes. At least today was turning out to be mighty fine. Mighty fine, indeed.*

Chapter Fifteen

Chloe's heart raced with each persistent knock on the tasting room door. No one interrupted tastings. For any reason. Ever. She stood pushing away from the half-finished nosings and walked with weak knees to the door, expecting dire news.

"Miss Tanner." Raelynn met Chloe's gaze with a grimace. "Miss Tanner, you have visitors waiting to see you. I have left them in the finance office."

"Who are they?"

"One gentleman gave me his card." She held out her hand. "They are from the Clearmont Management Company."

Chloe's posture stiffened. The name on the vellum card meant bad things. She turned to her team inside the tasting sanctum. "I apologize, I have been rudely interrupted. If possible, see if you can continue without me."

A short and stocky man with a round face and a pair of outlandish sideburns rose to greet her once she reached the finance office. "Miss Tanner. A pleasure to finally meet you."

"I'm afraid you have the advantage." She glanced at the card in her hand. "Mr. Flores?"

"Yes, Abraham Flores at your service, may I introduce my partner, James Philbin."

"Please, have a seat. Raelynn, will you wait in here

with me? Has my bookkeeper made you comfortable?" She pulled up another chair for herself.

"Yes, extremely so."

"What may I help you gentlemen with? Sales calls are prescheduled, as interruptions, particularly in the mornings, at a distillery are for the most part problematic. And my attorney keeps town offices."

"I can see you are a woman who is practical as well as competent." He gave her a huge smile showing lots of teeth, not unlike a nasty raccoon. Looking over at his partner he motioned for the packet in his hands.

"Miss Tanner, we are quite impressed with your ability to keep Tom Tanner's Whiskey Distillery afloat, regardless of all the tragedy and recent setbacks which have beset you. Taking the entirety of these events into consideration, meaning loss of revenue and product interruption in domestic and international markets, we are prepared to make you the following offer."

"We, Mr. Flores?"

"The Clearmont Management Company's Board of Directors and Partners." Mr. Flores passed a bound portfolio into her hand. "This is a contract asking for a percentage of sales for the next ten years plus one million dollars from Tom Tanner Whiskey in return for the water rights from the Wishbone Watershed, or an agreement to sell to us outright."

Chloe stood slamming the document on the desk beside her. "You are not serious?"

Mr. Flores flinched but continued with his terse discourse. "We are well aware you have a special affinity with your grandfather's business and would like to continue it, for that reason, we do not insist on an outright sale."

"Who are you?" She grasped the portfolio again. "I want names, who else is part of this elaborate hoax?" She flipped through the pages. She saw names she did not recognize in small print on the inside pages. She did however notice a revealing disclosure at the bottom of the income statement. "Your shareholders hold fifty percent of the company. Who owns the other half?"

"I am not at liberty to say. But it is quite common for land companies to have silent partners, for fear of pitting neighbor against neighbor. And I would be remiss not to emphasize—this is not a hoax. Your attorney and accountants, if fiscally responsible, should have apprised you of the possibility of a takeover attempt."

"Fear of pitting neighbor against neighbor. The only neighbor I can think of whom you might be referencing is the Kittrells'. I think you have an obligation to disclose here."

"Our relationship with the Kittrell's is not under discussion. I will leave you the portfolio and all our contact information. If, as you prefer, we can meet next to sign the contract agreement at your attorney's office in town. We are staying at the Star Inn. Alas, due to the fact we have other important business to attend to"— Mr. Flores stood and pulled out a heavy gold pocket watch—"we leave you twenty-four hours to consider."

"Or what?"

He opened his watch, noting the time before snapping it shut. "I believe you have been privy to some details documenting our substantial progress on the Wishbone Dam. My engineers tell me it will be a mere matter of days before the dam blocking water to your side of the Wishbone is complete."

Chloe stood motionless. Her voice shook in disbelief. "Get out of my office. Get off my property, now"—She pointed to the door—"If you don't leave right this minute, I'm going to go get my manager's pistol and start shooting."

The man bowed. "Any delay will convey a refusal. Please consider this very fair offer." He turned to his partner who had closed his briefcase, ready to exit behind him. After the two hurried out, Raelynn, who had stayed in the background listening to every word, shut the door soundly behind them.

Chloe grabbed the glazed pottery pencil holder from the desk and threw it across the room, it shattered into pieces. Fountain pens and pencils flew in every direction, falling and bouncing off the wood floor. "It's him. I've been played by Pen Kittrell." She stomped around the office. "He has to be the silent partner. No one else could pull this off," she shouted. "Why didn't I see this coming?"

She gave her head a deliberate, angry shake. She braced her arms on the top of the desk, her eyes stung from the magnitude of his betrayal.

I know when this started. When he found out I hadn't married Peter Tanner after all. He must have come to DC for the inauguration and planned to ask me to marry him. He did. It was his scheme to get my company all along. Jed Sanders stealing my whiskey was just a convenient red herring.

Chloe counted to twenty, then stomped down to the stables, tying the loose ribbons to her bonnet as she dashed to the last stall. "Jenks, Jenks, where are you?"

Her groom appeared from around the corner. "Yes, Miss Chloe?"

"I'm going to Kittrell's Distillery. And I'm in a hurry."

"Well, it will take a minute to get the horse harnessed to the curricle."

"Too slow, I'm going by horseback. Saddle Têtu." Her head groom mumbled something under his breath she chose to ignore. "I can get Bart to follow me if you don't want to accompany me."

"Hogwash. Hold your horses, Missy. I'm coming too."

****

She had never been to Kittrell's Distillery before. The hour's horseback ride over gave her time to cool her heels, enough that when she approached the distillery, she was struck by curiosity. How was Pen's operation laid out? A well-constructed conveyer belt funneled coal into the plant straight from their delivery depot. Two rick houses stood three stories high, adjacent to the back of the property. She determined both their distilleries made use of the easy access to water, however, it appeared as if Kittrell's bottling building was separated from the distilling area. It was noon, and many employees were taking advantage of the pleasant weather to lunch outside. A knot of women workers exited from what appeared to be his bottling facility. Could Pen indeed employ so many women?

She'd liked to have made a circuit of the whole property to study more, maybe incorporate some of their ideas; unfortunately, that item was not on her agenda. She passed the paddock next to the barn, Têtu whinnied. Patience was frolicking next to a new colt. *Good, with any luck I'll find him home.*

When she reached the red-brick residence, an

original square Greek Revival mansion with center columns and overhead balcony, she detected several additions, with their mixture of mismatched brick and stone. The home imposing, yet at the same time welcoming.

Footsteps came from around the house. Pen stopped in his tracks when he saw her, placing the ax he was carrying against the brick foundation. He was dressed in a coarse cotton shirt with open collar and sleeves rolled up and well-worn trousers.

Chloe caught her breath at the sight of him, tall and handsome in rough casual attire. She released her horse's reins, sliding off Têtu without Jenks' assistance. As her groom led the horse to the stable, she coughed before fumbling with the buttons at the neck of her shirtwaist dress. Her heart was beating a little too fast. *Why, oh why, does he make me feel this way?*

"I need to talk to you," she said thrusting up her chin.

Pen's turquoise eyes danced, and his smile—a crooked one at that—was devastating. "Why certainly, I'm sorry"—he motioned to his appearance—"I wasn't expecting company today. Was chopping wood."

"This is not a social call. Where can we go to speak in private?"

"Let's go into my library."

Library. Why had she never imagined Pen's home having a library? From the brief sketches she heard about his father, one thought the only reading material to pass the man's eyes was a contract with multiple zeros at the end of the starting number. Pen motioned her through the front entrance into the hall before pulling open massive oak pocket doors to the right.

Mahogany bookcases lined three of its four walls to the twelve-foot ceiling. A subtle dove-gray striped silk wallpaper pattern flanked the two long, skinny windows with their interior plantation shutters on the front of the house. Comfortable leather armchairs rather than stuffy horsehair Victorian settees were positioned next to each other. A portrait of a favorite horse hung with pride, books and newspapers laid open from recent reading, and large throw pillows spread about lent the room an embracing and well-used atmosphere. An inviting tray of whiskey decanters and cut-glass tumblers was placed on an ebony secretary desk. In another world, she'd like to curl up on that couch resting by a cozy fire with a whiskey in her hand, and Pen…She shook her head. Deciding it best to get right to the point, she asked, "Are you blackmailing me?"

"What?"

"I had a very surprising meeting this morning from two men who represented the Clearmont Management Company and a private partner. Are you the private partner?"

"Why would you ask such a thing?"

"As you are my lone neighbor 'similarly situated,' and since you have made no secret of wanting control of my company, it makes sense."

"You've made an erroneous conclusion. Yes, I'd like to run your company, control it if you will. If that were the only way I could keep those robber barons away. I'd fight tooth and nail before I'd let you sell out to someone who would turn Tom Tanner's Tennessee Whiskey into another carbon copy alcohol distiller, akin to a one-owner conglomerate like Standard Oil." He rubbed the back of his neck, grimacing. "Hell, I'm the one trying to help you keep it. Why do you think I showed you the pictures of the dam?"

"To get me to fold. To warn me. Like all the other things, the explosion, the shooting, the threatening notes."

"Whoa, what's this? Why have you not told me? What other things? What threats? I mean, I knew about the shooting and explosion, that's when I got Will."

"Got Will?"

He ducked his head, shaking it from side to side before looking up at her and giving a sheepish grin. "I didn't want you to come to any more harm. I had someone recommend him and had Milo hire him."

"Of all the..." Never had she been so maddened. She stomped around the room, fisting her hands, wishing she were in her own library, she knew for sure which vase she'd throw at him.

"What threats? From whom?"

"I don't know. They were marked 'X'. I thought it was simply someone who objected to whiskey."

"I wish you had told me." He exhaled a long breath.

"But you asked if I still held fifty-one percent of my company, why?"

"Because if you did, they'd have to answer to you, not some unknown or greedy Yankee. Don't you remember, I said we could fight this together. Please tell me you turned them down like I did?"

"They met with you?"

"Yes, last night. I refused their offer. I assume you had the same one?" He reached over to a colossal roll-top desk and retrieved a familiar burgundy portfolio. Her eyes were blurred with anger, she took the document with unsteady hands when he passed it to her. He picked up a business card. "A Mister Abraham Flores? You met him as well?"

Chloe was so stunned she slumped into the nearest chair. "What about 'the project' you and Sanders were working on?"

"I have no idea what you are referencing?"

"Right after I fired Sanders, I found a letter from you, thanking him for agreeing to 'the project.'"

Pen ran his hand through his thick hair, his brows furrowed. "The only thing I ever remember Sanders and me agreeing on was when we built the exchange room above the courthouse to post world whiskey prices."

Well, that blew her last theory of Pen and Sanders being in cahoots to undercut her to kingdom come. "I'm shocked. Up until this moment I suspected you of this all along."

"Me? Even the explosion?"

"Yes, you were the one person who had dynamite." She noted the pained look on his face. "Milo believed the blast wasn't meant to create as much destruction as it did, and, without question, not to hurt anyone."

"I swear to you, I would never do such a thing. Chloe, I told you before I'm not the enemy. It's not me you have to worry about. I have definite proof now, and it's not a bridge. Come look at these?" Pen walked over to the desk and pulled several photographs from a stack. "I hired a professional photographer to take these, I got them yesterday. These were taken at the Wishbone from the same spot you and I rode to a couple of days before the race. You can see the scaffolding of a dam."

"My word. It is a dam. And they'd have done this, cut off our water?" She looked back at him. "It wasn't just a threat, it's real?"

"It appears that way."

She rubbed the sides of her forehead with the palms of her hands. *Dear God.* She stared without seeing, too shaken to focus. Leaning forward to study, in more detail, the pictures, she asked, "What are we going to do? This has to involve a lot of money to go to such extremes."

"Not in this case. They used convict labor which is dirt cheap. Just had to make it look bad, show the threat was there. They figured you thinking a dam was being built would be enough for you to give up and sell out to them. But if they finished it Chloe, without water, they'd ruin us in days. I'm beginning to think Clearmont Management is a front for a trust trying to take over our distilleries."

"A trust. Oh my God, Pen. In Boston, there were terrible fights. Riots broke out. People died."

"They can't squeeze us out like oil or sugar by offering lower prices on their whiskey, because all whiskey is not the same. Their lone choice has been to blow us up or buy us out. But that's not worked. Their backup plan, I imagine, was to dam our water.

"Right now, here in middle Tennessee, we're impacted the most, because we need water to make our product. But there must be other communities in the state being threatened by someone trying to come in and take over their waterways. We need to get our lawyers on this. And it looks like it's going to take us all the way to Nashville, to the state capital, for this fight. We need to be ready."

"They told me I had twenty-four hours to decide. Period," Chloe said.

"We'll get an injunction. We have to work together on this, you understand?"

We have to work together. Did this man have a clue how difficult that was going to be for her? To be constantly in his presence. The mere proximity to him made her squirm like a worm on a fishhook. She had no choice. They had to work together, to fight the factions trying to destroy the very essence of their lives. Too late now—to walk away or try to ignore what the future held.

Drat it all. Her face heated as intimate thoughts of him flashed in her mind. She took a deep breath, stood up, pulled back her shoulders, and looked straight into his beautiful eyes. "Very well then, how would you like to begin?"

Chapter Sixteen

"Welcome to the Cumberland House. We hope your stay with us is memorable." The manager of Nashville's new palatial hotel spoke with pride puffing out his chest. Reports of guests being struck dumb upon entering the luxurious lobby with its marble columns, statuary fountains, silk upholstered chairs, and thick carpeted wide staircase were easy for Chloe to believe.

"Several flower arrangements have been delivered to your room, ma'am, and these cards are addressed to you." He passed the envelopes to Chloe and motioned the porter to take their bags after handing over their keys. "Anything you might need to make your visit more accommodating, please don't hesitate to let us know."

How she wished she could have had the hotel manager at her side for the past three weeks. Law case review after law case review, the telephone calls, the late-night meetings, the arguments, the interviews, the testimonials, were a blur. It would have been one of the most exciting times of her life, except for worrying what could happen if things did not go their way.

All their investigating and deep dives into what Clearmont was intending finally forced her New York stockholders and attorneys to sit up and take notice of who was actually running Tanner's. Their calls to her seeking answers and reassurances left them in no doubt.

She was not a figurehead—indeed, she was the very one responsible for the distillery's day-to-day operations and the successful transition of Tanner's after the demise of its founder.

She and Pen, their respective attorneys, Tanner Whiskey and Kittrell's Distillery et al merged their collective resources and put together a vigorous campaign to eliminate any attempts to block water from flowing downstream from the Wishbone watershed. Their investigation revealed Clearmont Management, an out-of-state entity, was indeed a trust, and was behind the attempted takeover. Fielding phone calls, accepting telegrams, organizing files, and taking notes—Chloe had helped wherever she could. She'd watched Pen covertly as he perused through leagues of documents looking for cases that supported their cause. Her heart sank as she realized once their fight was over, she would have no excuse to be in his company for hours on end without a viable pretense.

The onslaught of phone calls and telegrams to legislators, politicians, and other well-placed persons enabled their suit to be one of the first addressed in the upcoming congressional session. Miraculously, they were placed on the August calendar along with another party with a similar argument from the western part of the state.

"A calendar scheduling is not a guaranteed win." Pen had reminded her again, as they gathered in the hotel lobby waiting to go up to their rooms. They had ridden the train in from Oak Hollow that morning to be there in time for Pen's speech before the Land Management Committee. "I know what I will say, but there is no accounting for the power of others thinking their private property rights are being threatened. You can take a look around this hotel lobby and tell not everyone here is going to be on our side."

They walked toward the elevator and Chloe handed Bridgette her room's key and a duplicate of her own. "You must be on the floor above me. Bridgette, after you get settled, will you come down to my room and take out my blue silk? I'll wear it to dinner tonight."

"Yes, ma'am." The lift doors opened, and the two ladies entered.

"Pen come on."

"You both go on up. After an hour and a half on the train, I need some exercise. Knock on my door, Room 613, when you're ready to leave for the hearing."

Before pulling the door shut behind them, the attendant glanced at Bridgette's excited face. "Have you ever ridden in an elevator before?" She tucked her chin down. "At our grand opening last year, we would have townsfolk come ride in our elevator like it was a Ferris wheel at the county fair," the attendant bragged.

When they reached the sixth floor, Chloe squeezed Bridgette's hand. "Dinner is at eight. Come down before then to help me dress. Wish us luck at the hearing." She stepped out in the hall with the bellman and walked past Pen's room, the porter unlocked Room 615. She handed him a tip after he carried in her bags.

Late afternoon sunlight filtered through the huge windows. The room was tastefully decorated with less of the opulence and heavy Victorian style of other hotels she had stayed in. The scent from three huge flower arrangements threatened to overpower her. She tossed the envelopes she carried on the hall table, plucking one of the cards from the flowers. It was from one of her distributors wishing her success. Before trying to read another, she walked to the windows and drew back the drapes to open a window for some fresh air. She stood a second, taking in her view from the sixth floor. From this height, she could see over the warehouse rooftops to the bustling business sector of First Street to the swirling river below. As she removed her hat and placed it on the dresser, she noticed a connecting door.

I'll count to twenty, that should give him enough time to get there, she said through gritted teeth. *Twenty*. She pounded on the door. Pen took his time opening it, standing there giving her a wide-eyed look, smiling in amusement, but not saying a word.

"Did you know these rooms had connecting doors when you reserved them?" She shook her head, answering her own question. "Of course, you did."

"You look wonderful without your hat on. I've wanted to take it off all day," he said changing the conversation.

She walked into his room, noticing it was a twin of hers. "What, no flowers?"

"Apparently your reputation as the beautiful new owner of your distillery proceeds you. I'm sure you have a number of admirers from far and wide hoping to meet you."

She turned back to him, giving him a once over. Did he not know how pleasing his own appearance was? He had had his hair cut and his mustache was neatly trimmed. The charcoal gray suit he wore fit his muscled body like a glove. She brushed her sleeves up and down. "It's time to go. We can't be late for your speech."

"You know, we might have time for..." his gaze took in her eyes then drifted down to her lips.

There was a moment's pause. Neither said a word. She sensed her cheeks reddening. *Oh, for pity's sake.*

"I'll leave by my door and meet you in the hall. Be sure to bolt the connecting door, as I will on my side," she said exiting through the controversial door. When they met in the hall, Pen took her arm and walked her toward the stairwell. The lift bell sounded as they passed.

"Perfect timing," Chloe stood aside to let Pen open the conveyor door.

For a brief second, he hesitated, then stepped in front of her to pull open the door. They entered the empty elevator. When the doors closed behind them, Pen pressed the lobby button. The lift descended two floors at a slow pace, and then shook to a stop. The doors remained shut. Lights blinked off. Without warning the elevator dropped two more levels, stopping with a force that plastered Chloe against its corner. She gasped at the somersaulting feeling in her belly and sought to regain her equilibrium. Running her hands across the interior walls of the dimmed conveyor, she attempted to locate the operating buttons.

"Don't." Pen yelled before knocking her aside with one strong arm. "I'm sorry," he said as he lowered himself to the platform floor.

She reached down and felt for him in the dark. He had slid against the back side of the elevator. She touched his head, it was tilted forward and bent down between his knees.

"Pen?"

"I'm all right. It only lasts a few minutes," he

muttered. His body jerked, then began to shudder.

Chloe slid down beside him, placing both arms about his shoulders. With care she pulled his right hand into hers. "Feel my heart, it's beating like crazy too." She placed his hand to her chest. "Concentrate on my heartbeat."

Clanging echoed from above, rattling the whole compartment. Help had to be coming. Pen lurched again, but she held fast to his hand. She moved it to cover the curve of her breast and leaned in to kiss his cheek. He didn't turn away. She tightened her arm around his shoulders and waited with him for the bout to pass.

Pen's shakes slackened, his breathing slowed. Little by little, the tremors diminished altogether and he grasped her with both hands and pulled her tight to him. She sucked in her breath. She wanted to ask him what had happened but concentrated on helping him. Taking his hand, she squeezed it, then held it to her lips to kiss.

Screeching emitted from cables and pulleys above their heads followed by the flickering of the lights indicating a rescue was underway. Little by little, the elevator descended one more floor to the lobby level and the lights came back on. They helped each other to their feet and were able to present to stunned hotel management and assorted onlookers the picture of mildly disturbed guests as the elevator door opened.

The manager stepped forward. "I am so sorry. Mr. Kittrell, Miss Tanner," he said in a shocked voice as soon as he recognized his distinguished guests. "May I offer assistance in any way?"

"Do you have a private place we can go for a few moments?" Chloe asked.

"Yes, step this way. My office is to the left." They walked the short distance to a room behind the elevators. "Would you care for some water, sir, or something more substantial?"

"Yes, thank you," Chloe answered for Pen as he took a seat by the door. She lifted the pitcher from the serving cart and poured the liquid.

"If you would"—Pen spoke—"find my coach driver outside. He should be waiting to take us to the capitol. Please tell him we will be out shortly."

"Certainly," the manager said in a relieved voice.

When they were alone, Chloe studied Pen's flushed face. "I can go by myself. You stay here."

"I'm all right. I'll be fine."

Shaking her head, she wanted to tell him he didn't look fine. He accepted the drink she offered with steady hands, however, and appeared to have made a miraculous recovery as soon as they exited the elevator.

"Your cab ride to the capitol is waiting, your driver said to be in no hurry." The manager relayed as he stuck his head into his office door.

"We'll be leaving in a few minutes," Pen said, startling both Chloe and the manager. He stood and walked over to the drink bar and poured some of his own brand of whiskey from the choices available. He took a measured sip. "Are you ready?"

On the short ride to their destination, there was no time to puzzle over Pen's behavior in the elevator. Chloe kept any questions she had to herself. *How many times had this happened before? Had he ever seen a doctor about it? Was he, in good conscience, all right?* And Pen offered no explanation. *I'll sort it out later.*

Waiting at the lower entrance when they drove up

was one of their attorneys whom Chloe recognized. "Finally, you made it," he said when he spotted them. "Follow me."

The usual crowd of politicians, cohorts, and bystanders loitered around the door to hearing room number eight. Their lawyer walked the two of them around to a side hall, and they entered the hearing through another doorway.

"You're the second speaker," he said as he deposited them on the first row.

"I prefer to go last," Pen said, his lone deference to gain more time for himself.

The distinguished Land Management Committee Chair, sitting between the U.S. and state flags and flanked by the other committee members, gaveled the hearing to order as soon as they took their seats. The first speaker was Clearmont's company attorney. His appeal fell on familiar lines, wanting to distance themselves from any 'takeover' or trust language, they aligned themselves under the property rights mantra. The audience listened with politeness but did not acknowledge a particular preference for what was being argued.

The second speaker, from West Tennessee, did not have a suit, but joined the argument due to similar recent occurrences in their region. Their hope was to help establish precedence. He argued private property rights must not infringe on the trade of entire communities. His argument, that closing off access to a crucial lake and its tributaries, robbed fishermen of their livelihood. The restless audience, composed equally between property owners and business representatives, made it difficult to gauge which way their sympathies lay.

Chloe pushed her shoulders back and pasted on a smile, hoping she exuded more confidence than she felt. She gave Pen her most optimistic smile when he rose to speak. The stakes were so high. He glanced her way, bestowing a smile of his own, then commenced speaking, movingly and with conviction. It was hard to believe minutes earlier he had been racked by some kind of panic attack. There was no other way to describe it.

"Our great state boasts plentiful natural resources," he said in a calm deep voice. "The overwhelming majority of us in this room attribute our birthright to the very nature of what Tennessee has to offer. It is why our forebearers came here and remained here. It is why newcomers choose to settle here. From these natural resources, Tennesseans have created, with the sweat of their brows and the brains in their heads, bountiful produce such as corn, cotton, and tobacco and man-made products like wine and whiskey."

"Amen," someone called out.

"The latest inventions and cultivating method—whether you agree with them or not, allow the proceeds to give us a quality of life we enjoy. Better roads, better schools, better hospitals. In this state, we are each connected to the other by water—once that connection is blocked—our days are numbered. The question is—when one entity declares property rights over a natural resource and refuses access, whether it be a lake brimming with fish or a stream providing power—should we all suffer?"

"No." A voice in the back shouted.

"Not fair." A spontaneous cheer burst from the

crowd.

"In Tennessee, if one entity controls the water—they control you—therefore confiscating your right to life, liberty, and the pursuit of happiness," Pen concluded.

"Freedom!"

"God bless whiskey!" One emboldened spectator shouted.

The Chair gaveled the audience quiet, then gaveled the discussion to a close. It was motioned and seconded to take an immediate vote on *Residents of Oak Hollow, Tennessee versus Clearmont Management, Inc.* The critical vote to determine the company's rights to dam the Wishbone. The vote was thirteen to one.

Cheering erupted from the gallery.

The attorneys from the opposition approached Pen's side. "We withdraw any offer made to secure your companies and will abandon our work on the Wishbone. It is yours to dismantle in any manner you wish. Congratulations on your victory."

"Wait, your silent partner? His name?"

"A partnership no longer exists. Null and void," the attorney announced then withdrew.

Seconds later Pen absorbed pats on his back and punches to his shoulder.

"No one stands between Tennesseans and their whiskey," shouted another partisan.

Journalists jostled and elbowed their way to him to snatch a comment, before scrambling to Printer's Alley to write their stories. Crowds continued to shout hurrahs as they exited the hearing room, their attorney blocked the throng, allowing them to sprint to their waiting cab to transport them to their hotel.

Word traveled fast. As they entered the Cumberland's lobby, people were waiting to welcome Pen back like a conquering hero.

"Well done, son," A man with a full face of whiskers and a pinstriped suit congratulated.

"Terrific job. They say you could have heard a pin drop when you were speaking," a jubilant citizen declared.

"We've got the entire Hermitage Room reserved for our celebratory dinner tonight," another boisterous supporter announced as he grabbed Pen around his shoulder and stuck a cigar in his pocket.

"Yes, we'll do dinner. Then I'm done for. It's been a long day," Pen told them before whispering to her, "You go on up and dress for dinner. I'll stay here and entertain these gadflies a bit."

She gave him a questioning look before he patted her arm. "I'll be all right."

Chapter Seventeen

Smiling men and women nodded and stared at Chloe and Pen. Glasses raised to them in their honor as they entered the private dining room. Some held their glasses to their lips while others downed their toast. Men clapped their hands on Pen's back, the women batted their eyelashes, tapping his arm with their fans. It appeared every politician, lobbyist, captain of industry, socialite, assorted military officers, and newspaper reporter had garnered an invite to the dinner signifying the start of the legislative session and the celebration of its first legislative victory. The victory honoring the true 'liquid capital' of the state, whiskey.

"Ready?" Pen asked as he pressed his hand against her lower back. Squeezing one more person into the hotel's banquet hall looked impossible.

She had been ready long before he knocked at her door at eight to escort her down the stairs to the hotel's common area. Listening through the connecting door, she unlocked her side. When she heard him enter and shuffle around his room, her anticipation mingled with relief. She was still worried about him, though he showed no signs of this afternoon's bewildering distress. Was he putting on a good front, for her, for others?

"Yes, into the fray." She wished she did not have to be surrounded by another huge crowd. She smoothed her hands down her sapphire blue dinner dress, taking a deep breath. Eighteen pearl buttons secured the front of the low-cut wasp-waisted silk gown with its charming demi train that swirled flirtatiously when she walked. Bridgette had parted her hair in the middle and drawn it back in large waves to a high coil emphasizing her slender neck and ornamented it with a twist of more pearls.

She tugged Pen's offered arm close to her chest. His gaze took in her revealing bodice, then her lips, and up to her eyes, sending fluttery sensations to her stomach.

The toasts of congratulations started as soon as they entered the room and did not end as they wound their way through the expansive chamber. She glimpsed Pen under her lashes for the hundredth time, not only men hovered about him, but a good number of women lingered in his line of sight. Attractive and available.

Once seated, men stopped by their table. Talking and sometimes shouting over the waiters serving their guests the main course. "My good man, have you ever considered entering politics?" one man asked as he slapped Pen on the shoulder.

"Thought for a minute, it was a young Andy Jackson up there leading the troops," boasted one of their own attorneys.

How she longed to have him to herself. To make sure he was safe. To make sure he was all right, that he had the rest he needed from a taxing and unusual day. She scanned his face. There was no recurrence of another episode like the one he had experienced earlier, however, there was no guarantee in the clamor and press of the bodies in the packed room that another might not occur.

During dessert, a trio of men were so bold as to hint that the two of them should combine their distilleries. She twitched her nose at the pungent tobacco scent one man blew over her bare shoulder. As if on cue, Pen rose and placed his napkin down as the last waiter left. He lifted his tumbler and saluted his dinner partners. "Friends, advocates, supporters, I'm leaving on the first train home tomorrow. An unfinished business concerning a dam bent on destroying an entire industry must be addressed." He scooted back from the table then circled around to her. "Miss Tanner, may I escort you out?"

Chloe rose, blushing hotly, said goodbye, and ignored the knowing looks from the faces at their table while Pen spoke to the head waiter at the door.

"Thank you, thank you, I thought we'd never get away," she whispered to him as they exited, although embarrassed to the extreme by the obvious implication of their leaving, and together, before anyone else.

"What? I thought you'd be mad at me—preferring to stay and flirt a little longer with the gentleman who owned those sugar refineries down in Cuba?"

"The man in the red tie?"

"Yes, the man ogling your chest so long, I thought I was going to have to take him out."

Her laughter trilled the empty hallway to the elevators and stairs.

At the elevator, Pen stopped. "You go ahead, I'll meet you at the top."

"Not on your life, Penland Kittrell. As long as we stop on each floor's landing for me to catch my breath a second, I'll be fine walking up with you," she assured him. "Come on."

She pushed through the heavy doors of the staircase access and skipped up the first flight to the second. At the landing she caught her stomach, laughing, and she breathed in so deep her bosom was in danger of overflowing her low-cut bodice within seconds. Following on her heels, Pen made an effort to grab her when she ducked and scurried to the third floor.

This time he was faster, and when they reached the landing, he pulled her into his arms. He lowered his head to kiss her just as a door slammed down the hall. Giggling, she took the opportunity to escape and ran up to the fourth floor, losing a shoe in the process. She stood, out of breath, at the top of the stairs watching him approach her, carrying her lost slipper.

"Cinderella, I believe I have found something which belongs to you," he said smiling.

Her heart pounded so hard, she could not move. Pen leaned in, dropping the shoe and gripping her possessively. "I'm here to collect my reward." His lips touched her cheek, then sampled her neck and shoulders with cool kisses.

"I can't breathe. I feel like I'm being squashed to death." She tugged at her waist.

"Good, I've been wanting to undo these buttons all night," he said as he stretched to unbutton the first pearl, brushing her chest with the back of his hand. A heartbeat later his mouth was on hers, tasting, thrusting, quickening with a gentle stroke of his tongue. "Tell Bridgette to go on to her room, I can get you out of these clothes faster than she can any day," he whispered, fumbling with her bodice.

She tilted her head back, wanting to press her body next to his. Wanting him to rip all her buttons off. Each kiss, each caress sent her pulse racing. Another door opened, she moved from his grasp and stepped out of her other shoe.

"One more floor to go. And bring my shoes," she shouted as she sprinted up the last set of stairs. She ran the length of the hall, stopping when she approached her hotel room door. She buttoned up her dress and waited there expecting to say goodnight to Pen before knocking to allow Bridgette to let her in.

When he caught up to her, the elevator bell chimed with the door opening.

"Your slippers, madame," Pen said as he passed them over to her, then addressed the young bellman walking their way. "Thank you, perfect timing." He then knocked on her door before he turned to unlock his own room to let the bellman carrying the champagne carafe and glasses into his room.

"Miss Chloe?" Bridgette questioned opening her hotel room's door.

"Miss Tanner, would you care to join me for a toast to celebrate our good fortune tonight?" Pen asked as he passed coins to the waiting attendant. "Ah, Miss Bridgette, I believe I heard you have the rest of the night off."

Bridgette gave Chloe an uncertain look.

"Thank you, Bridgette, I can manage by myself tonight."

"If that is so, milady, I'll be off. I've already packed your bags and hung your traveling clothes for tomorrow." She bobbed a brief curtsy leaving the two of them in the hall.

"I'll never be able to face Bridgette again," Chloe said as she followed Pen into his room.

"Yes, you will." He passed her a flute of champagne. Just as she took a sip, the sky outside lightened with a flash from a distant thunderstorm.

"I hope it does more than thunder, we need the rain." Pen poured himself a glass as a few raindrops spattered against the hotel window. "A welcoming scene to watch, however."

He turned to her and lifted his glass, reflecting her. "A very beautiful scene indeed. A toast to us."

"To us." She smiled and took two sips while gazing out the window. "I can't stay. You know why."

"Yes, you want to get out of your tight dress. Let me help you." He placed his flute on the table and gathered her in his arms. She struggled to get away from his snuggling attempts, but not before he had undone three buttons.

"Pen," she said as she swatted away his hand. "It's been a long day, you said so yourself, we have to leave early, you need your rest...after what happened in the elevator today."

"Ah, yes, I remember someone kissing me—" he leaned in and kissed her ear "—and yes, I remember someone placing my hand on their heart." He tugged at her open bodice and placed his hand above her heart, undoing another set of buttons.

Clasping her dress back together, she said, "Be serious. As I said, you need rest."

"Humor me. Let me be your patient." He swung her around. She landed in his lap as he sat on a cushioned chair. "Pretend we are at your hospital training classes."

"First off we would never be caught sitting on patient's laps," she smirked.

"The nurse matron just exited the room to investigate the loud banging of bedpans in the hall."

She giggled as he asked, "Show me, Miss Chloe, how you roll bandages?" he gathered the hem of her dress lifting it up.

"Careful, my champagne." With quick purposeful hands, he reached up under her skirt, releasing the garter on her left leg. "Stop," she pleaded, sliding her drink onto the table before pulling at his hand.

Pen expertly rolled down her silk stocking to her ankle. "Am I doing it right, Miss Chloe?" He nuzzled his neck against hers. "Can you please kiss this patient? It would make him feel so much better."

She found it difficult to think. "I can't breathe."

"Yes, I'm sorry, I said I would help." He held her tight with one arm and brought the other from back under her skirts to undo more of her pearl buttons. Chloe squirmed in his lap, wondering if she was being attacked by a sorcerer weaving a magic spell over her body. She smacked away his hand again, which speedily returned up her skirts and rolled down her other stocking. He delivered soft gentle kisses, which trailed the length of her neck, then back toward her mouth. He scooted her into a more comfortable position on his lap as his hand under her skirt moved higher and higher.

She wanted to jump up and run, wanted his assault on her senses to stop, yet she returned his kisses. His head moved down to her chest where one hand had pulled away her lace-trimmed summer corset. Encouraged by her involuntary murmurs, his playful mood dissolved. He drew a ragged breath as he kissed his way to a bare breast, slow and deliberate. Chloe arched her body, allowing even greater access. No magician could transport her to such a state as this. *Oh, my word.* The reality far surpassed any of her most arousing dreams.

The days, the three long weeks working together side by side, had taken their toll on her. Her denial of him, her wishing her feelings for him would go away, disappeared as fast as the bubbles in her glass of champagne. The scent of him as she laid her head against his neck, the scrape of evening whiskers, of a starched collar, and sweat mixed with sandalwood banished any more thoughts of leaving him. She sighed as she nudged her head into the crook of his arm.

His hand beneath her skirt sought her core, she cinched her thighs together. One tug pulled her silk drawers down, his fingers advanced up her limbs, then retreated, waiting her out. She curled her fingers, grasping his jacket, lifting her leg ever so slightly. His groan of approval was followed by more slow fondling and caressing. Too weak to hold out longer, she slid her legs apart. His fingertips stroked, kneaded, and circled her essence.

"You want me," he whispered. She lifted her knuckle to her lips then pressed her teeth to his neck, squirming again to ease the throbbing in her innermost part. Back and forth, up and down, never entering her fully, every movement arousing shudders of pleasure. She wrapped her arms around him, the sound of her pants and moans echoing in her ears. She twisted above him, digging her hands through his scalp, fisting her hands in his hair, wanting to beat his chest, his shoulders, his back, but he was relentless in his torture, skillful in his teasing.

Her whole body trembled as his hand glided over and inward, touching the most sensitive part of her. His thumb pressed there. Like a master gardener discovering the center of the bloom, he was deflowering her in an altogether different fashion. A floodgate of desire unfurled, spilling over in blissful pleasure.

"Let go, Chloe. Let go," he urged. She tumbled over the edge, wilting into an abyss so deep it took her several moments before she regained clear thought. She dared to meet his eyes.

Her muscles useless, she could not sit up straight. It took great effort to tug her skirt down. She stood on wobbling knees. Inhaling deeply, her constricted lungs let out a scant breath. She breathed in again, then once more, before her breaths resembled normal. He stood too, waiting for her to make the next move. Looking deep into his eyes, she curled her fingers about his hand. She wanted to have the wanton joy of giving him pleasure herself.

"Come to bed?" she asked.

A slow, wicked smile spread across his face. He gathered her in his arms and carried her to the edge of his bed. Kissing her between breaths, whispering, "I thought I was going to have to ask Bridgette to leave us alone on the train to Nashville so I could ravish you, I wanted you so much. When you walked in my room through the connecting door this afternoon, I swear," he said as he slipped her dress off, "if we hadn't had our meeting at the capitol, I was going to take you right then and there. These past weeks, being so close to you but unable to touch you, have driven me crazy."

She laughed between kisses, assisting him in removing her clothes, so he could start on his own.

"I want you completely naked," he said, as the last article of clothing dropped from her shivering body.

She brought her lips to his as he joined her in the enormous hotel bed. She pushed him to his back and lowered her mouth to his shoulder. She bit hard, savoring the male taste of him. Continuing her exploration of him, she smoothed her hand across his chest, kissing his muscles and flat nipples as she went. Pen reached for her hand and curled it about his stiff maleness. Knowing nothing of technique, she played inexpertly with his male anatomy. She heard his short intake of breath.

"Kiss me here. Like I kiss you."

She lowered herself to his abdomen and gently stroked, then kissed the silky-smooth hardness. Branding him with hot lazy circles, her tongue flickered around him, then with one languorous sweep, took him inside her mouth. His heavy muscles twitched and tensed as he offered a ragged growl of approval.

"I have French letters—" he gasped as his muscled arms reached down clutching her shoulder to haul her up to him.

"What?" she asked attempting to sit up and straddle him.

He flipped her over on her back, climbing over her body, pinning his over hers. Blindly, he nuzzled her breasts, her stomach, her welcoming triangle. Her insides quivered as he pressed his maleness against her. Pleasure spiraled, as the fire she started burned out of control. She should be accused of arson.

"Oh, hell," he muttered, he flexed his hips sliding deep inside her. She wrapped her arms around him, arching her back, welcoming the havoc he wreaked on her. He was careful not to crush her with his powerful thrusts, but she was thankful he didn't stop. As the storm outside pelted fierce raindrops against the hotel windows, she curled her fingers into his shoulders, unwilling to break his rhythm. She held him tighter and tighter, until his body convulsed with the release of intense shudders, and his groans muffled silent into the thick pillows.

They lay in a tangle of sheets, watching as an occasional lightning-flash lit in the distance. Pen stretched out, cradling her in his arms.

"You're all right?" she asked.

"You have to ask?" he teased, nibbling her shoulder. "I meant to make love to you. That's why I brought the French…"

She placed two fingers on his lips and didn't let him finish. "I'm glad it happened." Smiling at her own satisfaction, she kissed him, content in her knowledge that she had indeed pleasured him. Emboldened, but choosing her words with care, she asked. "Pen, why did you collapse today in the elevator? Can you talk to me about it?"

He sat up and scooted off the bed. He went over to the occasional table and grasped the champagne bottle in the carafe and poured himself another glass of the still effervescent mixture. After taking a huge gulp, he returned bedside. "Would you like some?"

She shook her head. He took another swallow, then hovered over her prone body and kissed one nipple with the cool comfort of the liquid left in his mouth.

"Quit trying to distract me," she said sitting up in the bed and tugging the covers over her body.

"I'm not. And you, my dear, are the ultimate meaning of distraction. I wish I could put you in my back storeroom like those doctors back at your school."

"Pharmacists," she quickly corrected, sneaking a mischievous smile.

He took another drink and set the glass on the bedside table before climbing in with her again. Looping his arms about her, he drew her to him.

"I'm just working up false courage. I think I'm claustrophobic. In truth, Chloe, I know I am. I can't ride in an elevator without an attack like the one I had today. Most of the time I never enter them. If I do, I exit in seconds. And today, when it dropped three floors, and we were trapped…"

His voice caught. And he took a deep breath before releasing her and sitting up in the bed. "I think it started when I was ten. Your brother and I went exploring an old, deserted cave we should never have gone in by ourselves. We'd been there before and thought we knew the way out through a crevice. Anyway, some stalactites collapsed on us. We dropped down to another ledge. I don't know how many feet lower. Everything was pitch black, piles of rock, afraid to move. We could hear water, nothing else. It was one of the triplets—Clark McCoy, who saved us. It was a miracle. He was a few feet behind us when the ledge caved in, and he was able to crawl out and go for help."

He shivered, and Chloe sat up and wrapped her arms around his shoulders, her breasts pressed against his back, she kissed his neck.

"They got us out after two days. Me and Noah, we

never talked about it to anybody ever again, not even to each other."

"Pen, New York has buildings twelve stories high now. We had a meeting in one of them on the tenth floor when we prepared for my trial against the shipping company. You can't just think you can climb every building's stairs. My friend from Boston, she visited Paris during their World's Fair and went to the top of the Eiffel Tower in the elevators. The tallest structure in the world. I'd like to go. You'd like to go too, I'm sure."

"Yes." He dropped a kiss on her shoulder.

"Speaking of Boston, they have doctors there for everything."

"I'm not going to any doctor," he said straightaway. His eyes gleamed in the dark room as he turned and took her in his arms again. "I have the best cure in the world for what's ailing me right now."

****

Pen woke before dawn to rattling carriage wheels, jangling horse harnesses, and the blast of a steamboat horn from the riverbank below his window. He rose and carried Chloe through the connecting door to her bed. As he laid her under her covers and kissed her brow, he contemplated their future. She was a novel experience for him. Taking him somewhere he'd never traveled. He'd never opened up to a woman like her before, sharing his worst fear. And it was a tall one. One, for the first time in his life, he determined he had to face.

He returned to his room and gathered her clothes, chuckling when he found her slippers, remembering how she lost them. He placed them under a chair in her room, giving her one last look. His fairytale princess, his sleeping beauty. He was taking her on a journey too. Not one she had ever been on before either.

****

Steam evaporated from the already sweltering streets of Nashville. Last night's storm did little in the way of alleviating three months of drought conditions or decreasing the heat level over the mid-state. And little did last night's passionate lovemaking dampen Chloe's longing for something she had yet to obtain. Rubbing her palm over her heart, she peeked out from under her summer bonnet and studied the man in front of her.

With instructions to Bridgette to get their luggage loaded on a coach and meet him at the rail station on Broadway, Pen left their hotel and did not reappear until time to board.

"No point in wasting time getting orders on destroying that dam," he told the two of them as they settled in their train compartment for the trip back to Oak Hollow. "I made two telephone calls this morning. Both to our lawyers. We do not want word to get out to the general public yet of what we plan to do."

She studied Pen's handsome face as he sat engrossed in three editions of the state's morning papers, keenly searching for any scrap of news recounting yesterday's success at the capitol. She could be a discarded umbrella on the train seat opposite him for all it mattered. Did she feel slighted or ignored by his inattention following a night of making love? She shouldn't be. One thing she had learned from her brother, father, and grandfather, the male species could only concentrate on one thing at a time.

Chloe leaned back in her seat after removing her hat and gloves. Lost in thought, she still basked in the afterglow of last night. Vivid, alive memories danced in the forefront of her consciousness.

I'll not become your mistress, Pen. I need to tell you this.

Yet she wanted him to be *her* lover. Did one send an attorney over to exact the terms of scandalous propositions? Oh, to be more worldly, more sophisticated. To know how to navigate the intricacies, the particulars, the details of such an arrangement. As expected, reality crept in. They did not live in New York or even Boston. They lived in a small town. And already negative opinions concerning the distilling of alcohol percolated nationwide. If her name were tied to an illicit love affair—she would jeopardize the standing of her whole company.

When Bridgette left their compartment to get them all coffee, Pen looked up from the newspaper he was reading in his lap. "They reported we won our appeal but little else. The authorities must collect the convicts. We can't allow them to delay and give them time to finish the dam emplacements."

She smiled at him, pushing back her thoughts along with her bruised feelings. *Soon I'll broach the subject of us forming a liaison. Later—once things are settled. After this whole debacle is behind us.*

"If whoever instigated this were to stop the water flow even one day, it would be disastrous," Pen said. He swept his hand through his thick hair. "Because of that, we should be prudent, not be seen together until we have a sound strategy on how we want to proceed. I don't want to give away our plans before we're ready to move. We can't hinge our success on what happened yesterday."

"I don't understand," Chloe said. "I thought Clearmont Management withdrew?"

"They did but never divulged their silent partner. There's too much uncertainty floating around, too much potential for something to go wrong. When this is all over—Chloe…"

"Pen, we've been honest with each other from the beginning. Our distilleries come first."

His forehead wrinkled as if trying to read her better. He leaned over to take her hand when Bridgette returned with coffee. "We'll talk later," he said, shoving his hands in his pockets before staring out the window.

Chapter Eighteen

It was cool in the early light of the last day of August. Pen rode over to the wooden bridge and dam, which now spanned almost the entire length of the Wishbone Watershed before it split in two, flowing east and west. It was here at the top of the 'Y' where Clearmont Management and its co-conspirators had planned to strike their lethal blow. His jaw tightened, then he gave a quick disgusted snort. Too close. Damn too close, he thought as he surveyed the well-constructed structure. A mere fraction of the dam had been left unfinished.

It had taken every ounce of his energy, every second of his time in the past three weeks since they won their case, to have the last of the convicts removed and set today's activities in motion. Little time to see Chloe, and no time to allow him to court her as he should now that she no longer suspected him of destroying her distillery. His horse's ears perked up at the faint sound of wagon wheels and hoof beats of other riders converging on the same embankment. Pen had predetermined the date and time of the destruction of the dam, the act to preserve and protect the distilleries vital water supply for hopefully generations to come.

Milo Knox and the three McCoy's had acquired enough mule power, chain, and rope to dismantle and pull apart the dam that threatened their livelihoods, their way of life, their very existence. As the men positioned the animals and tied off rope, Pen looked up and saw Chloe ride in on horseback along the track of the riverbank. The exhilaration of her gallop and the rush of morning air brought color to her cheeks. Laughing, she reined in next to him. A hyper-awareness of her, as anytime she was in his presence, made his sprinting pulse race faster. He moved closer, letting their two mares nuzzle each other. Oh, how he wished he could pull her down from her horse and do the same.

It wouldn't be long, he thought. He looked about. Members of the community, neighbors, employees, all well-known to him, had heard through the grapevine what was happening. In singles and in groups, they made the steep climb from town to see for themselves. He turned and spotted Chloe's mother in one of the wagons rounding through the clearing.

"Who's the little boy sitting up with your mother on the wagon?" he asked.

"He's my heir."

"Your what?"

"I forgot, I haven't seen you in so long."

"Chloe, I'm sorry. There's been so much to do." For a second, guilt crossed his face. "You're not mad at me, are you? When this is over, we'll go to Nashville again…"

****

Did he just say that? Like I'm his whiskey woman? Willing to drop everything to trounce off to the big city for some forbidden love affair? The suggestion in his voice was unmistakable. Her chest tightened.

"Well, to be frank, if you cared to hear about anything other than mules for days on end, I would have told you my mother's recognized Dillon as Noah's son. No one knows yet. It's not been finalized. She hoped to adopt him, Raelynn Brown refused. But she's agreed for her son to take our last name."

He rubbed his forehead with the back of his hand, then Patience snorted when some of his own workers dropped a rope of heavy chain in front of him.

"Times like this, you wish we had some dynamite," Milo said stepping up.

"Sore subject," Pen said, looking sideways at Chloe.

"Just saying, we might be here all day trying to pull this thing down. And I sure as hell don't want to see a mule get wrenched into the river. If we loosen pylons and they're still tied to our mules, the yank back will jerk us in and then there'll be hell to pay."

Pen surveyed the area again. "I see the truth in what you're saying."

More and more people congregated and milled around the east side of the riverbank, the designated staging point. Chains, rope, iron hooks, heavy harnesses, and six mules were grouped in a cordoned area. Instructions were meted out to the men recruited to help. Another full-size wagon clamored around the bend. Two giant Clydesdale's labored to pull the heavy vehicle over the rough terrain to the staging area.

"Who's that?" Chloe asked Pen as she observed an old man in the driver's seat who looked like one of the dwindling war veterans with his excessively long beard and ragged gray coat.

"Hell's afire if it ain't Homer Burns. Biggest moonshiner in the state, don't you know," exclaimed Milo.

Chloe and Pen watched the old man with a pair of henchmen by his side lumber in with a mammoth cart. They drove to the drop-off point where the resources had been gathered for the dismantling. In the back of the wagon sat a huge wooden thirty-gallon covered tub.

"Come on, I want to introduce you. You have to meet him," Pen said with a throaty laugh.

"Hey there, thought you might need some help," Homer announced, acknowledging Pen as casually as if he were invited to attend a local barn raising before turning his attention in Chloe's direction.

"Chloe Tanner, I'd like you to meet Homer Burns," Pen said with a look close to idolatry.

"Nice to meet you, miss." Homer doffed his ragged hat before giving Pen an obvious nod of approval.

"What'cha got in there, Homer?" Milo asked hobbling over to the wagon.

"What'cha think? One-hundred and forty proof," the old moonshiner answered.

A bystander whistled.

"Thank the Lord, someone with a lick of sense thought this thing through. No diddle-daddling along." Chloe's foreman stomped over and looked inside the wagon.

"Heard tell you was trying to do this with just mule power, figured you'd need something with a little more kick to it." Homer's two men dismounted from the cart and then unhooked the tailgate. Pen's disbelief became excitement, even envy, then appreciation, for the offering from the county's old reprobate bootlegger.

"Can't thank you enough, Homer."

"Don't see your local sheriff around." He squinted looking about.

"State marshal deputized him yesterday to help take the last of the convicts on the train to Brushy Mountain Penitentiary."

"Well, good. Figured you didn't want to wait all day for a hole to burn through that damn dam. Brought along something to give it an extra boost." The old man guffawed at his own joke, then bent over and pulled out a sack from under the buckboard. "Gotcha some gunpowder in here to help it go."

"Well, let's get started," Pen said joining in on the hasty modification of their plans.

He turned to Chloe. "Help move all these people back, pull the wagons out of the way, take all the horses on up the crest." He swung off Patience and handed the reins over. "Take her up there as far as you can. Tie her to your mother's rig. We are going to have one hell of an explosion."

Once she and her mother had moved their wagon to safety, Chloe dismounted Têtu, tying Patience and her horse to the vehicle. She stood motionless, staring at the furor of activity around the wooden dam. It looked so much stronger and better constructed than the drawings and pictures she had seen of the dreadful structure.

Taking hold of the side handles, four men hoisted the barreled tub Homer had brought in with concerted effort. It was important to position the pure grain alcohol in the dam's most vulnerable spot. Chloe grasped her fist to her hand, afraid to turn away as she watched Pen help maneuver the tub to a secure position in the center point of the dam. She began praying, muttering promises as she strove to control her shivering.

"In five minutes, this dam is going to have a hole

blown in it the size of an elephant," Milo shouted stumping up to join her.

"Back up," someone screeched. Children passed her on a dead run as others, like her, stood still as statues, watching as shredded rope tied to the container of pure grain alcohol was lit.

The tattered rope fizzled, flashed, then ignited a blazing trail toward the waiting moonshine and gun powder positioned precariously in the dam's midsection. A fiery explosion roared with such a force it knocked the nearest bystanders to the ground. The torturous efforts succeeded as gallons of unimpeded water crashed through the new opening. Broken timbers groaned then dragged, in cascading lurches, the evil apparatus down, freeing the Wishbone.

Chloe's mind swam. Sparks and a blinding haze filled her vision. *Where was Pen?* A lean dark shape emerged through the smoke, doffing his favorite hat, slapping irksome embers from its brim. The face, which turned up searching for her in the crowd, at last located her. If ever she wondered what he looked like as a boy on Christmas morning, it was at that moment.

"We did it." Pen's voice echoed in her still ringing ears. "Got to stay for a bit of clean-up. If all right." He tipped his hat to her mother when he reached the side of her wagon, "I'll ride over to Tanner House tomorrow. Something important to say."

Her mother gave her a slight shake of her head.

"No, Pen. I'll be in town," Chloe said. "Our attorney from Boston is coming down. We've got some family documents to sign, and we're hopeful he'll announce good news concerning selling stock shares."

"Pen, let's put off a visit until next week. When

things are a little more settled," Regina suggested. "Right now, so much is happening, and I know you have tons to do. We should have some news to share with you by that time as well."

Ignoring the congratulatory guffaws and shouting, Pen nodded and untied his horse. He took one more look at Chloe as if he searched for something more from her. She wanted to erase the questions between them, but today was not the time.

"Go enjoy the celebration," she said smiling. "You deserve it!"

Chapter Nineteen

"Mr. Owens, Mr. Owens," Chloe shouted as she steered her curricle toward the entrance of the Star Inn, Oak Hollow's historical hotel. Her attorney agreed to visit from Boston to free her from having to take another trip East after giving him assurances Oak Hollow was less humid and more congenial than Boston in September. He had prepared documents releasing shares of Tom Tanner's Tennessee Whiskey stock to be sold to raise capital for the distillery's renovations. The funds she desperately needed after the explosion. His other important responsibility, certifying Raelynn's boy changing his last name to Tanner.

"I'm so sorry, I'm late. I meant to pick you up at the train," she apologized.

"No matter, my dear," he said as he descended the steps and reached to pat her hand.

"Did you see my cousin? Did Maggie come with you? Her mother is hosting dinner tonight for us at her house. We were to ride over to their house together."

"No, when I didn't see you, I walked to the hotel myself."

"Mr. Owens, if you don't mind, I'll drive to the depot to see if she is waiting for you not knowing you had departed. The locomotive is still at the station, she may think you are on board and haven't left yet. I'll return to pick you up."

She gave him a quick smile before driving down the block. After tying up, she darted inside the terminal. She passed the ticket counter, turned the corner to check the boarding platform, then stopped as if she ran into a brick wall. In front of her, just inside the terminal door, stood Pen in what appeared an intimate embrace. His back was to her, but she would recognize his figure anywhere. He was hugging a woman with wavy brown hair, bestowing gentle kisses to the top of her hatless head.

Backing up on shaking knees, Chloe turned to exit and fell headfirst into the arms of her cousin.

"What is it? What's wrong?" Maggie grabbed her arm. "Tell me." Chloe opened her mouth, but nothing came out. She shook her head.

"Tell me." Maggie tightened her hand.

"Pen, with a woman, I've seen her before," she mouthed, attempting to pull her cousin away from the waiting room, not wanting to stay in the terminal another minute.

Shaking her off, Maggie hurried around the corner. Within seconds she returned. Grabbing Chloe's arm again, she thrust her outside. "They didn't see me," she said, once they were on the sidewalk, her face white as her dress, "But I know who that was. Come on. Let's get out of here."

"Wait, wait. Who was it?"

"Daisy Pemberton."

Stone-faced, Chloe drove in silence at a snail's pace back to the hotel to retrieve Mr. Owens. She kept her gaze on the road and made no attempt at small-talk after they squeezed her attorney onto the carriage's bench seat and headed to Maggie's townhouse two blocks away. Not sure how much her cousin guessed about her feelings for Pen, and nor how intimate they had been, she stayed close-mouthed. She raised her face up to the sky. *Thank you, thank you. It's twilight and no one can see how red my face must be. Or how much my heart hurts at this moment.*

"Mr. Owens, let us drop you off at the front door, I'm going to help take the gig to the barn. Our mothers are inside waiting to welcome you."

"Maggie, I remember that woman now." Chloe slapped the reins to drive the gig down the driveway alley as soon as they deposited her attorney. "She was at the horse race. Pen was holding her so hard on the track, I could almost feel it. She's his old sweetheart, isn't she?"

"Yes."

"I suppose I shouldn't say old. She can't be much older than me."

"Chloe, how deep are your feelings for Pen Kittrell?"

"He asked me once in jest to marry him. But it was because he wanted my distillery and thought it would be the easiest way to acquire it. I think he now wants me to be his mistress."

Her cousin clasped her hand to her face as if she had heard blasphemy. "No."

Chloe bit her lip. "Maybe he truly loves her. He said he had something important to tell me yesterday when we blew up the dam. Maybe he was going to tell me then. Oh, what a fool I've been. Maggie, I can't face him now. Knowing what we…" she stopped. *What we did together. Oh, my mercy.*

"We'll go to the river house. He won't know

you're there. We can remain there and hide as long as you like until we learn the truth." Her cousin patted her hand in sympathy.

"I thought he just desired me, no one else." She caught Maggie's intake of breath. "Oh, Maggie, please don't be shocked. I didn't think he'd ever be like my father—married to someone upstanding—yet seeking out other women for his bed." What a time to dredge up old memories. She collapsed against the back of the carriage seat. The sense of betrayal compounded her hurt.

"You're upstanding. He could marry you." Her cousin stared at her. "You never answered my question. Do you love him?"

Chloe wiped tears flooding her eyes. *Do I love him? Yes.*

How could she not love Pen Kittrell? How long had she pushed back, squelched, and shushed her inner voice—telling her the memories she replayed in her head, of not only their intimate moments together but of all their time together—was what her heart yearned for. Why, of all people in the world, could she not recognize love? Discovering love was like her days as a novice whiskey taster, you were not an expert—but at that moment—you knew when you experienced something special.

For the rest of her life, she would be searching for that gleam, that special smile, the way he looked at her which made her want to melt. She fisted her hand to her heart. She loved how he cared for his whiskey business not just for himself, but for those around him. Loved how he took care to make sure she was safe, how he believed in her, wanted her to succeed. She loved how he made love to her. How he had awakened a passion in her she did not know existed.

Maybe she had misconstrued what she witnessed at the train station. Was it too late? Too late to tell him she loved him.

"Yes, yes, I love him," she answered her cousin. "It just might not matter now."

I love him. No denying it. How long, or when? She shook her head. But she would never be the mistress to a married man. She witnessed firsthand what kind of a heartbreak that brought to her family. *Oh, why does this have to happen to me?* If there is another woman, better to break off any relationship now, before things got too complicated. Before my heart completely breaks.

"Wait until we hear what's what. Let's see if a betrothal is announced," Maggie said. "Either way, come with me to the river house. The trip will give you time to decide how to handle everything."

****

In the next few days, no news circulated about pending nuptials attached to Pen Kittrell's name. Maggie's mother, who would have heard any new gossip, had nothing to report. A subdued Chloe returned home. Two very vague notes waited for her on her bureau. Both were requests from Pen asking to come visit, no reason why included.

Several times at her cousin's house, Chloe wondered if she should approach Pen face to face? He had to be keenly aware she was avoiding him. Maggie insisted on her waiting Pen out. However, the suspense was killing her. She walked down to her barrel warehouse past the carpenters and other workers rebuilding and renovating her distillery. For once, so distracted with thoughts of Pen, she ignored all the hammering and nailing, leaving the supervising to Milo and Corbin. She was done waiting.

Sunday morning dawned bright and clear, a sure sign temperatures would climb multiple degrees throughout the day, still a perfect day for riding. Chloe had Têtu saddled then asked Corbin to ride with her. They rode south and crossed the Wishbone at a spot so shallow since the drought, the water did not even touch her boots while wading through. A flock of geese flew overhead. Not long before they would start their annual migration to warmer climates.

"There won't be any fall foliage this year if we don't get some rain soon," she said as she trotted alongside Corbin. "Your family's home is near here, isn't it? Might we drop by for a visit?" Was she hoping to gather information regarding Pen from Mrs. McCoy?

"Yes, speaking of family, look coming our way. It looks like both my brothers are riding over to us."

"Morning, Miss Tanner." Caleb raised his hat the same time Clark did. "Have you ridden past Monroe's yet?"

"No."

"Well, there ain't much to see. He's plowing over his cornfield. Says it's all dried up. Just getting it ready for next year. Too late for any yields this fall. We heard about Sawyer's crop burning. Don't know which is worse."

"Going to be a long winter for some 'round here," Clark said.

"How's everything at Kittrell's, Caleb, Clark? How's your owner?" Chloe asked.

"The same, maybe a little bit more ornery," Caleb

offered.

"Where is he? I haven't seen him lately."

"Rides over to Piney Flats a lot."

"To see Daisy?"

"Daisy? Who? Hell no. If he's seeing a woman over there it'd be Fatima."

Chloe pulled back on the reins.

Caleb shot Clark a look. "Well, we got to get back, Mother's expecting you for dinner tonight, Corbin. Ma'am." He lifted his hat to her and turned his horse around, leaving her with their flustered sibling.

Chloe felt her face turn red pepper hot. Her general manager politely looked away.

"It ain't what you're thinking," he said. "She's not a sportin' woman. She's a spiritualist. Possesses special powers some think."

Chapter Twenty

Damn, why didn't I notice this earlier? Pen had seen the train glide down the tracks the day before when he was out riding his property. It was one of the specially designed Pullman cars fitted for a number of robber barons making their annual treks to the south once cooler weather started to invade the north. But September wasn't November. A rare occurrence.

He turned Patience back around and trotted to the other side of the tracks where the railcar had been pulled over to the side until ready to engage again. The gold signet 'T' embellishing the side of the elaborate black railroad car and likewise its ostentatious caboose was hard to miss. He clenched his teeth so hard his jaw ached. The cars could only belong to one person, Peter Tanner.

Bells rang from the Baptist Church on the edge of town as soon as he passed the depot. But no sounds came from carriages, wagons, men, women, or children crowding the forever bustling streets on a Saturday in Oak Hollow. The sidewalks typically thick with townsfolk were abandoned. After dismounting Patience, he changed his mind about visiting the bank first and strode toward O'Malley's saloon.

"Long time, no see, Kittrell. Not too much of a celebrity to share a drink in the company of people who knowed you since you were knee-high, are you?" the bartender goaded.

"You know me better than that, Fletch. Give me a shot of your best, which better be mine. Speaking of company, where is everybody? This place is deserted," he asked, taking in the empty bar and unoccupied tables and chairs. "And what's the story on the fancy train. Peter Tanner's, isn't it?"

"It's Peter Tanner's all right. Guess it was true about Tycoon Tanner being sweet on one of them Tanner women. Most of the locals are at the big church wedding this afternoon."

Pen froze momentarily, then doubled over as if he'd been sucker-punched. He squeezed his eyes shut. *By God, she went ahead and did it.* A September wedding. He scrubbed his mouth, then picked up his drink and tossed the fiery liquid down. "Let me have another."

"Sure." Fletch refilled his glass.

Pen knocked back the second drink, threw a silver dollar down, and stormed out the swinging doors. Bumping right into the bank's head teller, Pen grabbed the man's arm.

"What time's the wedding?" He angled his head toward the hill.

"Wedding's over." The teller announced. Pen sagged against the saloon's wood siding. "Everyone's headed over to Clayton's now."

"Clayton's?"

"Yeah, for the reception at her parent's house. Nola Clayton married the Bondurant boy." He patted Pen on the sleeve. "They're big teetotaler's, I'd say that's why you didn't get an invite."

She's not married! He gave an ugly laugh. And

slapped the surprised man on the back. *Yet.* A burning sensation tore through his gut and black splotches flashed in his eyes. A desire to vent, to let her know, once and for all, what he thought of her, was now. If ever in a moment's reflection he honestly thought he loved her, he doubted his sanity. *Holy shit and shit fire.* Must have been out of my frigging mind. No wonder she had been avoiding him the past weeks.

Turning, he sprinted down the sidewalk, jumped off, and untethered Patience.

"Mr. Kittrell, Mr. Kittrell," someone behind shouted his name. He recognized one of the railroad porters. "Got a note here for you," the out of breath man gasped. "Was supposed to hand deliver it. Was on my way to your place when I spotted you. Holy cow. Going to save me half a day seeing you here in town."

He handed over the folded paper and gave a broad grin when Pen tossed him a coin. "I'll mosey over to O'Malley's now, as I got extra time." He tipped his hat and fled.

Pen looked at the letter in his hand. He didn't recognize the writing but knew it was hers. He stuck the letter in his shirt pocket then leaped in his saddle, gave Patience one swift kick, and headed for Tanner Place. He knew what was in the letter. An, *I'm so sorry, but I'm getting married to Mr. Wealthy after all* note, what they called a 'Dear John' letter during the war.

So, she now had a Tanner heir, conveniently provided by her brother Noah. Only thing she lacked was piles of money. I'm not just going to give Chloe a piece of my mind, he decided as he galloped out of town. I'm going to make sure Peter Tanner appreciates precisely what kind of Jezebel he's fixing to tie himself to. Might be right now he doesn't care, but by the time I'm finished with him, he will.

Pen's pace did not lessen until he reached Three Mile Bridge. As he approached the overpass, he recalled how he felt when he first learned someone had shot at Chloe at that very site. One hitting her groom. He slowed Patience to a trot, exhaling a deep breath. A train whistle sounded in the distance reminding him of his mission. His breathing returned to normal, and the flashes of anger dwindled. Reality crept in, making him realize the hostility he felt toward a rival was misplaced.

She deserved to be loved. Deserved to have children, and for those children to have a father. Not like hers, or his either. *I'll not stand in her way. If she is determined to go through with this horrible decision, she's going to know she had another choice.* And that was him. He would make sure she knew he loved her, completely and utterly, loved her.

Pen crossed the bridge and cantered around the creek bend another half-mile, pulling his horse up short when he spotted Chloe's abandoned curricle in the middle of the dirt road. From his saddle, he looked about, then dismounted. Cautious, he walked around her vehicle.

"Easy, boy." Pen stroked the mane of the lead horse. The gelding tossed back his head as Pen checked both horses' harnesses. Everything appeared to be in order. He strode to the side of the road leading to a shallow ravine below. Visible drag marks ran through the dirt.

"Chloe, Will? Hey. Anyone?" He scanned the slope following beaten-down branches through which something had fallen or been thrown. A patch of blue stood out beneath the underbrush. His heartbeat raced. Scooting sideways through the blackberry brambles, he darted his gaze around the area. Guardedly, he approached the spot, easing, step by step, down the steep incline. His knees weakened, almost buckling underneath him when he recognized Chloe's driver tangled in the weeds.

"Will?" He leaned down and turned the man over. Blood saturated his pants leg.

"Kittrell, that you?" the man moaned, looking at him with bloodshot eyes.

"Shit fire. What happened? Where's Chloe?"

"He got her. The scum bastard," Will spit out.

Pen collapsed back among the hillside briars as a sudden feeling of heaviness overcame him. His voice cracked. "Who?"

"Jed Sanders."

Replaying in rapid-fire the events that had taken place over the past few months, wishing what he was thinking could not be true, he asked the obvious. "Was it him all along?"

"Yeah, had to be. And he was just waiting. Took us by surprise. Blocked the road on horseback and had his rifle pointed right at her. Knew I wouldn't take a chance of her getting hurt. Had me get down from the rig and that's when he shot me, damn it." He gave a hoarse laugh. "Missed my gut and shot me in my leg. Knocked me off balance and I rolled down the hill. Reckon he thought I was dead."

Pen took his knife and slit the man's pants, making strips of the cut off fabric. "Let me tie this around your leg to stop the bleeding. Why in hell were you two up here?"

"Miss Chloe said she got a note, said she had to come alone. Couldn't stop her. You go on. I'll be good. I know where he took her. Willow Ridge."

"Willow Ridge. Why there?"

"Perfect place for an ambush."

"Who's he going to ambush?"

"You."

"Me? What for? Don't answer." He finished a makeshift tourniquet on Will's thigh, then glanced at Chloe's bodyguard's colorless face. "It's revenge against me, I guess, for what I did, busting up the dam." He shook his head, wiping the sweat from his brow with the back of his hand. "But damn, Sanders must hate her something awful I reckon. A woman catching him stealing, then firing him in public. He wasn't going to forget that. Crossed my mind more than once he was behind damming the Wishbone. Couldn't ever figure out why Clearmont Management's boys would, all of a sudden, come down here to try and take over."

"Easy. Someone dangled a hell of a lot of dollar signs." Will grabbed his arm. "How'd you know to come so soon? Just been an hour since Sanders left. If it's a trap, which I'm sure it is, seems he's cutting his time short."

Intuitively Pen reached into his pocket and pulled out the note, the one passed to him less than an hour ago. He broke the seal and opened the letter. *"Come quick, alone. Willow Ridge. Chloe"* was scrawled on the page. The scribbled text, even if he had recognized her handwriting, could have been construed as someone's writing in a panic. It was a planned attack, with a pre-written message jotted down, then delivered.

One which would be sure to bring him, but one that wasn't supposed to be read until hours later.

Will clenched his wrist. "He means to kill you both. No doubt about it. Wants to send both your distilleries into collapse, hoping to pick up the pieces. Take my gun. Kept it under the seat box. He won't expect you yet. But be careful."

"I'll send help back for you."

"Don't you worry about me. Go save her fast. While you still got time."

Chapter Twenty-One

Willow Ridge. He hadn't been there in years. When he switched places with Noah that summer, he toured the planned site alongside Chloe's grandfather. The old man started his facility's relocation up on the knoll after a one-hundred-year flood came close to destroying Tanner's distillery. Like everything else after the Panic, the construction was put on hold.

Pen dismounted Patience at the stacked stone entry gate courtyard for the new distillery. Limestone blocks had been quarried, cut, and positioned to form the foundation for the new plant's construction. The vacant structure took on the look more of an abandoned city razed after a fierce battle. He scouted the rock groundwork and scanned the upper edifice. If it were an ambush, Sanders would seek the higher ground. The place appeared deserted. There were no horses or tracks to follow. A mockingbird flew out of her nest, startling him. He traced the perimeter, edging along the backside of the distillery's layout, he spotted Chloe's boot lying in the dirt. With caution he stepped over to retrieve it, keeping a lookout for Sanders the whole time.

A faint simper echoed fifteen feet away. He crept closer to the sound coming from within the half-constructed interior walls. He heard it again. The sound came from the large well dug in the rear of the site to provide water for mortaring bricks and for the workers themselves.

"Chloe?" he croaked out in a whisper.

"Pen, Pen? Is that you?" Her voice floated up, weak and feeble.

He hunched down then stretched out to skulk along the dirt floor until he grasped the edged of the circular hole in the ground. He leaned over and peered down. Chloe lay sprawled on her side down the enclosure some twenty-five feet below. Somehow, she had fallen or been thrown into the well's excavation. His whole body was consumed with anger and fear. His muscles tensed in knots. He reached an arm down, a useless act.

"Chloe, are you all right? It's me. I'll get you out."

"No," she cried. Her face was ashen white. "Go, leave me. He's out there. Jed Sanders. Pen, he means to kill you. He already shot Will."

"I've got rope, I'm going to fashion it so you can climb out."

"No, Pen. Leave me. Go. I can't climb." Her voice shivered. "I think I broke my arm. Feels like when I broke it before. Go before he shoots you. Hurry," she begged.

"Chloe, I'm tossing my jacket to you. Stay warm. My flask is in the pocket. Drink what's in it. Going to Patience to grab rope. I'll come right back, then I'm scaling down to lift you out."

A gunshot pierced the air and ricocheted against the brick wall in front of Pen. He ducked behind a barrier, then belly crawled away from the enclosure. From the direction of the gunfire, he calculated Sanders had gone to tie up their horses. Most likely, he was at the northeast corner at the high point of the ridge. Light glinted off what Pen was certain was gunmetal. Good.

The shooter was looking into the sun, maybe not sure of what he spotted. For a few minutes, Sanders might think he was still hunkered down with Chloe trying to avoid getting shot. That gave him two minutes or less to get around the ridge and surprise him from the rear before gathering storm clouds blocked the sun.

He reached down and scooped up a decent size rock and hurled it at the same wall where the bullet had shattered moments before. A reflexive gunshot burst in the same area once the rock smashed against it, giving him time to duck and run around the back of the ramparts. The overgrown foliage and thickets covering the hillside allowed him to scamper up the incline undetected. Within minutes he reached the backside of the summit. A mere ten feet below him, Jed Sanders crouched behind a wall scanning the lower section with the sight of his twelve-gauge shotgun. Pen stood on the rock ledge and cocked his pistol.

"Drop the shotgun on the ground, real slow, then stand up and raise your hands," he ordered.

Sanders placed the rifle, with his right hand, in the dirt and stood raising his hands shoulder high. "Don't get tetchy now, you're gonna need me to help get that gal out of the well she fell down."

"You got two seconds to start moving your fat carcass over to where you tied your horses."

"All right, all right." Sanders grumbled, trudging toward the patch of scrub pines. Pen jumped down from the ledge and followed him, his revolver aimed at his back.

"You know you got me all wrong, Kittrell. I had you in on the deal from the start. Still time. Clearmont money boys were willing to pay me big as a silent partner. My idea, the Wishbone dam. I got other ideas. I got enough of your stolen dynamite left over to blow Tanner's to smithereens this time. We can get the little lady out and send her back to Boston. She'd be better off there; a city gal. Got no reason trying to run a whiskey business."

"Shut your trap, Sanders. Get the rope you've got tied to your saddle there and start tying a knot for yourself." Clouds blew in on a hot burst of wind, darkening the skies.

"You trust me?"

" 'Bout as much as…" A flash of lightning lit up the western sky, striking the gnarled trunk of the giant cedar steps away. The violent explosion sent shattered embers flying cutting off Pen's word and diverting his attention from his adversary as Sanders threw dirt, blinding Pen's left eye.

Pen swiped away the dust, stepping back a split second before the big man charged him like a mad bull, hurling them to the ground. Sanders had a good thirty pounds on Pen. Pain jarred his body from the larger man's impact. His breath whooshed out of his lungs, and his fingers slackened around the pistol grip. Sanders grabbed at Pen's right hand, the one holding the gun, and slammed it into the dirt.

Damn son of a bitch.

Pen threw a left hook to Sanders' temple and dug his boot heels in the hard clay. Bucking up, Pen heaved to his right to push Sanders off. Sanders tightened his grip and fought to remain on top. He seized Pen's shoulders with his massive mitts and pounded Pen's head to the ground. Jerking him up and slamming back down, intent on killing him one way or another.

Bright colors flashed in and out of Pen's consciousness, he struggled to breathe like a drowning man. Dazed from the bruising impact, he shook his head, determined to fight through. He grabbed Sanders' collar and smashed the pistol's grip on his assailant's skull. Not daring to release the gun, Pen delivered a left-handed knuckle punch to Sanders' chin. The man recoiled, spitting blood. Pen seized the moment and yanked his hand holding the firearm out of his attacker's reach.

Sanders' growled, clawing at Pen's throat, lunging for the pistol.

Pen pulled his free arm down and stabbed his elbow into Sanders' gut. The heavier man clenched the gun with one hand but let go of Pen's neck with his other and pummeled him without mercy in the side. Gasping for air, Pen sucked in a huge breath. Pain shot through his ribcage.

An ugly fury rose inside Pen. Raw power surged through his body. *No way you'll harm one more hair on Chloe's head.* He curled his fist and punched the man's jaw.

A crack sounded. Sanders spit more blood. Grunts echoed inside Pen's head. Clenching his teeth, he wrenched his knee into his assailant's groin. Sanders cried in pain, slackening his death grip on the revolver.

Each man grappled for the upper hand, seeking ultimate control of the firearm. Sanders roared and head-butted Pen. The blow allowed Sanders to get both his hands on the gun, enabling the bulkier man to force the pistol beneath Pen's chin. Sanders contorted face hovered just inches above Pen.

Time slowed. Pen stared at his own death. No, he

refused to let the man win. It would mean Chloe's death. With herculean strength, Pen pushed the gun down with both his hands, lodging it between their chests. Sanders eyes bulged. Certain the muzzle was aimed at the big man, Pen squeezed the trigger.

Sanders went limp. Pushing the big man off of him, Pen rolled over, and picked up the gun. Spitting dirt and blood out of his mouth, he glanced at Sanders' body as he stood. Spitting was too good for him. Tamping down an overwhelming desire to kick the scoundrel, he wiped his eyes before scanning the sky.

Birds flew in every direction as a result of the gunshot. His ears rung and he could not hear a sound. Chloe—he winced, no telling what she was imagining. He looked up once again at the billowing clouds, dark and ugly, changing weather was rolling in. The summer had been a dry one, but flash floods came in fast to middle Tennessee.

He stuck his pistol in the waistband of his pants and limped toward the tied-up horses.

"Easy, boys." Pen tried to calm the skittish mounts. Grabbing the one rope off the roan pony, he unhitched it from the saddle. Not enough. He returned to Sanders' body, and stripped off his belt and pants, then took his knife and shredded the buttons to pull off his shirt.

He glanced back up at the threatening skies. Not much time. Water would start filling the well making a rescue more difficult. He sent up a speedy prayer. Sanders' rope and what he brought from Chloe's gig had to be enough to devise some sort of ladder.

He retraced his steps, picked up the shotgun at the ledge, then whistled for Patience. "Good girl," he said patting her mane as soon as she trotted up. He untied the rope from his saddle, not as much as he hoped but with what Sanders had, it might be enough.

Clouds mounted on the horizon, and the sun was setting fast. Hobbling as quick as he could to the well, he peered down. Chloe's white dress spread across the well's floor, but he barely made out her face as the encroaching storm made the late afternoon darker and darker. If she had passed out it would be even more difficult to extricate her.

"Chloe, I'm back." He tried to hide the panic in his voice.

"Pen," she sobbed, raising her head, "I heard a gunshot. I was so afraid."

"Sanders is dead. You're safe now. I'm coming down to lift you out."

"No, Pen. Don't try to climb down. Go for help. I'll be all right."

As he looked once more into the well, the familiar heart palpitations, trembling, and shaking started. The cylinder walls began closing around him. Scooting away, he clutched the two ropes he'd gathered and held them, not able to tie them together.

"Pen? Pen, are you still there?" Chloe whimpered.

Hearing the anguish in her voice was all he needed. "I'm coming down."

He forced himself to tie knots in the rope every three feet, using Sanders' belt and pants he constructed the makeshift ladder. He tied the rope around the iron staff imbedded next to the well and pulled hard to test its strength. Last, he secured the end around his waist.

Breathe in and out. Take deep breaths, focus on inhaling and exhaling. Re-center your mind. Remember what Fatima instructed. He looked around. *Name three things you can see.* Chloe's boot, the rope, Sanders' belt. *Name three sounds you can hear.* The storm, Patience's impatient stomping, and Chloe crying. *Name three parts of your body.* My legs, arms, fingers. *Stand up straight, your body will sense it's back in control.*

Jerking the rope around his waist, he checked again. He took a deep breath, ignoring the pain in his side and ribs. Satisfied, he started his descent, fingers tight on the rope. With every move, clumps of dirt and rock gave way. As he went lower, he wanted to retch but refused to let himself. His eyes gradually became accustomed to the darkness. A few more feet, almost to her.

Breathe, remember to breathe. He ignored the pain from his bruised ribs.

When he reached the bottom, with utmost care, he pulled Chloe into his arms. "My love, oh my sweet, sweet love."

"Pen." She lifted her face, and he kissed her hard. Reluctantly, he released her. "You're hurt," she said as she rubbed her hand down his face.

"It's nothing. Let's get you out of here. Does this hurt?" He managed to loop a sling around her arm he made from Sanders' shirt and tie. He knotted it behind her neck.

"No, but it smells awful."

"Another story. Can you piggyback me and hold on? If you can't, I'm going to have to climb with you over my shoulder."

"Kneel down. I'll hold on with my good arm. Are you sure you can do this?"

Was she afraid he didn't have the strength? Or that he would suffer another panic attack and shake so much he'd drop her? He turned, facing her in the remaining light.

"Chloe, you can trust me with your life. Nothing will stop me." He kissed her again before turning to help her climb on his back. He jerked the rope taut to test it once more. It had to work. "Ready?"

"Yes." She flung her uninjured arm around him and held tight. After one agonizing pull after the other, Pen got them closer to the surface. As he grasped the top, he turned to maneuver Chloe around and shove her to safety. "My arm, it's stuck, wait." She wrenched free, then gasped, "Pen, push me. It's okay, it's already broken. Push."

With her last command, Pen heaved her around and over his body until she was out of the well. He pulled up beside her and collapsed. Reaching out to her, he ran his hand over her face, arm, and waist, tugging her into him. The tingling in his hands ceased, his limbs light as air, and his chest expanded. The feeling of joy made him want to shout. He leaned down and kissed her like a man reborn.

"I love you, Chloe Tanner. And I want to marry you. There is nothing you need in life from Peter Tanner that I can't give you."

"Peter Tanner?"

"I saw his train," he said as he untangled then retied the makeshift sling.

She started laughing, in hysterical gulps. "You saw his train? He came to visit my mother. Did you not know he is sweet on her?"

"No, hell no, I did not," he said, and laughed ironically. "I thought you got in mind you preferred living in New York with your rich millionaire, not down here, especially now that you had an heir. Noah's son. A real Tanner to take over for you."

"Oh, Pen, how could you think such of thing?" She laid back in the dirt, a soft whimper escaped her mouth when she jarred her arm.

"Shush, darling." Alarmed at her obvious pain, he reassured her, "I'm going to get help."

"Pen, I...you don't have to marry me. Marry Daisy."

"Marry Daisy?"

"I saw you together at the train station. Maggie told me about you two."

"Daisy Pemberton? Daisy Pemberton is married. I met her at the train station on the way to her mother's funeral. Her son had been in a carriage accident, so her husband stayed behind with him. I knew her mom and met her to support her."

"So you don't?"

"No. And why the hell didn't you say something? Is that why you've been avoiding me? I sent you two messages. You never answered. I can see now we need to do a much better job in communicating. In the meantime..." He stood and walked ten feet away, without warning, he shot the pistol in air three times. "Hopefully, the sound will send help our way. Can you sit up? Let me see if I can at least get you on Patience."

He whistled for his mare. "This is going to hurt a bit when I put you up. Got anything left in my flask? Drink it down if there is."

After hoisting her up in Patience's saddle, he found the near-empty flask in his jacket, but Chloe had already drooped her head on his horse's mane. "I'm coming up behind you." Holding his breath, he eased himself up trying his best not to jostle her when pain stabbed his ribs.

Before they reached Chloe's abandoned curricle, they were met by three riders, and another coming from where they just left, Willow Ridge. With relief, Pen recognized Milo, Bart, and another stable hand from Tanner's.

"Hold tight. I'll bring Miss Chloe's carriage up from where we found her bodyguard so she can ride in it," Milo Knox said when he surmised the situation.

Corbin McCoy rode up to them from behind. "Miss Tanner, Kittrell. Damn glad to see you both. Took the back way into Willow Ridge. Saw Sanders' body up there on the ridge. I can understand a gunshot going through his chest, just can't explain why he had no shirt or trousers on."

For the first time in twenty-four hours, Pen's face stretched into a grin so wide, it hurt. "Long story."

Chapter Twenty-Two

By the time they reached Tanner House the whole structure was lit up like it was decorated for a Christmas party waiting for guests. Every window, every door was thrown open, waiting for the sound of, not for guests to arrive, but for their missing young mistress.

"We sent out an alert as soon as Jenks told us Chloe had left along with her bodyguard and carriage but no word to anyone as to where they were going," Milo said when they approached the gravel driveway.

Pen pulled to the front of the house, easing back on the reins. Chloe had fainted a few miles back. Her head lay across his lap as he drove the curricle home. They'd placed the wounded Will behind them and, with his added weight, the trek was slow going.

Bridgette rushed from the front door as soon as the carriage turned in the drive. Pen lifted Chloe's head up to his shoulder. "Help hold her while I get down," he said.

"Yes, Mr. Kittrell." She climbed up the other side of the coach seat placing her arms about her mistress.

He jumped down and reached over and gathered Chloe in his arms. "Show me to her room." Carrying her limp form, he followed Bridgette through the front door and upstairs. Her mother was already inside her room pulling down the bedspread and sheets.

"Her arm's broken, Mrs. Tanner, Bart's ridden for the doctor." He continued to hold her in his arms. "One of you want to get her shoe off? Lost the other one."

Bridgette unclasped the low boot and tugged it off.

"Bridgette, find a nightgown." Regina saw her own maid at the door. "Go heat up some water and fetch me cotton sheets to tear for a sling." She plumped Chloe's pillows before motioning for Pen to lay her on her bed.

Chloe murmured a faint groan as he laid her on her pillows, then he unknotted the makeshift sling, gingerly pulling it off.

"You're home now, Chloe, you're safe. I'm here," he whispered in her ear.

Her mother placed her hand on his. "Pen, thank you. You'll stay tonight. Run over to the annex, get cleaned up. I'll have some supper sent over to you."

Gripping the remnants of the cloth, which had served as a temporary sling, he peered down at his own bloody shirt, Sanders' blood. He glanced up at Regina, her flawless face appeared strong, her eyes clear and focused. He hadn't noticed earlier. And now she was like a mother bear protecting her cub.

He stood and looked at Brigette holding a white nightgown, and Regina's maid holding a stack of sheets standing in the doorway, and then back to Regina. Waiting for him to leave so they could get her undressed and cleaned up. Undress the body he had memorized every inch of, that he knew and treasured more than anyone in the room could possibly know.

Reaching down, he touched her hand, curling his fingers around her limp wrist, reluctant to leave her side. He wanted to take her back to his home. He wanted to be the one to undress her, to bathe her, to care for her arm. He could take care of her.

Glancing up, he blinked. Three sets of eyes stared back at him. God, he had to be an awful mess himself in his dirty and blood-soaked clothes. Taking a steeling breath, he brought Chloe's hand to his lips and kissed her palm,

He caught Bridgette's eye. "She's had some whiskey—I had her drink what was in my flask. Go easy on anything you give her." He sent a wary look over to Regina.

"I'll stay with her through the night, Mr. Kittrell, I'll not leave her side," Bridgette reassured him.

"Please don't worry, Pen. We'll take care of her," her mother said, escorting his reluctant self to the door.

Pen tramped along the hall and descended the stairs. Outside, the stable hands had already taken the carriage and his horse to the barn. He heaved a heavy sigh and trudged over to the annex, knowing Chloe's men would take excellent care of his mare. Inside, hot food and a coffee pot on a tray had been placed for him on the drop leaf table. Pen pulled up a chair and gave himself over to the small comfort provided for him.

He'd eat, then take a shower before walking back over to check on Chloe. Pen searched the chest of drawers in the room. He opened the top drawer and found items someone had forgotten or left on purpose. Inside was enough of Noah's clothes to select a clean shirt and trousers. There were several pairs of cuff links and a pocket watch he recognized. Noah had a son. He shook his head in disbelief. He placed the items back. These should go to him.

When carriage wheels sounded in the drive, he figured it must be the doctor. *I'll give him time to examine Chloe before heading over to her house. Need a short nap first.* He laid across the bed. As his head hit the pillow, the soft, clean smell of the linen reminded him quite vividly of the first time he spent the night in this bed.

"Oh, Chloe, my love," he murmured, shuddering once with the thought of how close he came to losing her. He fell into an exhausted sleep, dreaming deep dreams of Chloe happy, impatient, delighted, passionate, brave. Dreams which carried him through the night until long past sunrise the next day.

****

As he crossed the gravel path to Tanner House the next morning, the sheriff walked up from the barn.

"Ho, Kittrell, glad you're finally up," he said, rubbing his brow. "Seems like I got to get another statement from you for a criminal report, this time about a shooting,"

"Guess the boys in the stables told you the whole of it. If you don't believe me, you can question one patient." He nodded in the direction of Chloe's house. "She's got enough bruises and a broken arm to substantiate any of it."

"No need." The sheriff answered with a slow smile. "Been down to the manager's cottage and interviewed her driver already. Tough customer there. So it was Sanders spearheading it all from the explosion to the dam building?"

Pen nodded.

"You'd think outsiders would have figured out by now ain't no way to come between Oak Hollow folks and their whiskey. Wish justice was always served so swift. Tell Mrs. Tanner thanks for the coffee."

"Will do," Pen said, before encountering Bridgette standing on the Tanners' wrap-around porch.

"You might as well have coffee and breakfast too, Mr. Kittrell. Miss Chloe's sound asleep now. Had a rough night. The doctor set her arm, and within an hour, she brought on a fever. Cook made her some broth and we got her to swallow some at dawn. I think having something in her stomach helped."

"I'd like to see her if I may, just to know she's going to be fine. And please call me Pen."

"Let me take you up."

He stood at her door and peeked in. Regina reclined in a rocking chair on the other side of her bed. Her mother appeared to be napping, so he stepped away after checking on Chloe and slipped down the stairs.

"She looks more herself, doesn't she? She'll have some nasty bruises in a day or two, but nothing nobody will see." Bridgette blushed as soon as the words were out of her mouth.

Pen laughed at her embarrassment. Appreciating the fact she knew very well he'd most likely be seeing those bruises. "I'm going 'round to the stables to check on my horse. Want to do some riding for an hour or two. If you could make it possible, I would like to sit with her this afternoon."

"Yes, Mr. Pen." She bobbed.

"Bridgette, was Peter Tanner here?"

"He came to visit a couple of days ago, left yesterday. Took us ladies to town to see his fancy train. A bit lofty. Not for me. He's gone on to Florida. I think he's partial to Mrs. Tanner," she confided.

"So I've heard. Bridgette, do you ever miss Boston?"

"No, sir. I like living here. And it's a good thing, 'cause Miss Chloe says she never wants to go back."

He traipsed down to the stables in a lightened mood, juggling tangerines in the air. One check on Patience assured him of her well-being, when a familiar snort, then whinny, beckoned him from the last stall.

"Hello, Miss Têtu. How'd you like to go for a gallop today? Jenks, Jenks, you around?"

"Want to take Miss Tanner's mare out? She'd like it, very nice of you. Give me a minute to saddle her up."

Jenks returned with a blanket and his saddle. "I'll toss yours on her. If Patience won't mind." As he worked, Pen peeled the tangerines he'd brought with him from the breakfast sideboard and fed the pieces to Chloe's mare.

"Something about you girls, you sure do love your tangerines."

"Mr. Kittrell, I didn't get a chance last night to thank you for what you did for Miss Chloe. You took care to get her back to us in one piece. And I thank you."

"That's means a lot to me hearing that from you, Jenks. Between you and Milo, I guess I stand a distant third as to being a male friend of hers."

He shook his gray-haired head, "Wouldn't go so far as to saying that. No, sir." He winked. "A close third at least!"

Chapter Twenty-Three

It was late in the afternoon when Pen returned to Tanner House. He hadn't meant to be gone so long, but by the time he'd given Têtu a run for the money, he found himself near where the Wishbone split. Turning the mare, he galloped over to survey the area for the first time since they blew up and destroyed the dam. A lone hawk circled the restored riverbank, soaring high above the lazy current. Pen gave a silent prayer of thanks. The water level was still markedly low due to the drought yet—flowing fresh, clear, and unimpeded. Guaranteeing, at least, another generation of whiskey making.

After making his way to the stables, he gave Patience love pats, then strolled to the annex to clean up before visiting Chloe. The long afternoons, since mid-summer had come and gone, were growing shorter and shorter. He paused to scan the skies once again. The clouds had darkened but had yet to produce any rain.

He sauntered over to Tanner House, entering without knocking, and climbed the steep stairs two at a time. At Chloe's bedroom door, Bridgette sat in a heavy ladderback chair reading a book and blocking access to her room.

"Hello, Miss Bridgette is all well?"

Why yes, Mr." she paused, "Pen."

"I've come to pay Miss Chloe a visit."

"Well, as to that, Mr. Pen, milady was feeling so much better when she woke up from her sleep and had some soup, she asked to take a bath. Tired her out for certain getting her bathed while keeping her cast dry. Soon as her Mum and I got her back in her bed, Miss Chloe said she fancied to take a long nap and would we be so good as to leave her alone and quiet. So that's why I'm guarding this here door. Her mum's gone to her room and is napping too. Why don't you go to the annex, and I'll send word when she's rested and wants to get up? It shouldn't be long."

Pen sagged against the wall, frowning, he raked his hand through his hair. His heart felt like it was shrinking as he slogged down the stairs, swearing his limbs were shackled to leg irons. He kicked an apple size chunk of gravel as he tromped back over to the annex, missing by inches one of Mrs. Tanner's prized rose bushes. As he trudged up the stairs, a noise came from inside the bunkroom. *What now?* The sound definitely came from the other side of the door. Slowly, he turned the knob then pushed the door open. The room appeared empty.

Without warning a figure in white rose from the wingback chair and whispered, "I thought you'd never get here."

"Chloe, darling, darling." In three quick strides, he reached her, crushing her so tight she whimpered in pain. "Oh sorry, oh so sorry, my love." Releasing her, he smoothed her soft golden locks with both his hands, then pulled her close to kiss her forehead, taking in her particular scent of roses and oranges, which sent his pulse racing again. His mouth became dry and his muscles unexpectantly weak, so relieved he was at seeing her awake and alert. He struggled to find the right words. "Oh, Chloe, you gave me such a scare." His arms curved around her, holding her as hard and close as he dared.

Keeping her head on his chest, her eyes lifted to his face. "I'm sorry."

All of a sudden, her appearance dawned on him. He had to ask. "Did you and Bridgette plan this? Have you snuck away?" He held her out at arm's length. She blushed, then giggled, giving her dimples full reign before wobbling. She clutched his arm to regain her balance.

"Silly me. Here, sit down."

"I'd much rather lay down. Lay down with me, Pen, and hold me."

He pulled the pillows from the bed covers and placed them on top of the quilt as they lay facing each other. For the longest while, they held hands, staring at each other without blinking.

"Chloe, I don't know how much you remember about yesterday. I hope it wasn't too much, because I offered you the stupidest proposal you could ever imagine. And I'd like to start off fresh. Clean slate." He paused to gather his breath. "I'm not much of a poet, but I know I love you with my entire being. And I'll thank the angels above until I take my last breath for having you pick me out from your collection of mourners to make love to the day I first met you."

"Shush." She placed a finger to his lips, and with an embarrassed grin, tucked her head into her chest. "I can't believe I ever did that."

"Thank God, you did." He lifted her chin wishing she could see into his heart. "I can only guess the angels were happy with their 'Angel's Share' of whiskey from both of us. And desired to keep a good thing going. My darling, I can't imagine living my life without you. If you still want to run your company, I'll ride back over here every night to be with you until the next morning when I leave for work. But marry me. Please, will you marry me, Miss Chloe Tanner?"

Tears welled in her eyes. Her cheeks glowed as she returned his tight grip on her hand while waiting for her answer. "I would not marry you unless I loved you—so it is a wonderful thing I do. I love you with all my heart. I think I must have fallen in love with you from the very first night we spent together yet was afraid to admit it. Yes. Yes. Yes. I'll marry you, Mr. Penland Kittrell."

A warmth radiated throughout his entire body, stronger and more powerful than anything brewing in tanks sitting a hundred yards away. He kissed her face, combed his fingers through her golden hair, spreading the long locks across her pillow, and then bent and brushed with his lips her fluttering lashes again. He embraced her once more, careful not to put weight on the plaster cast, running from her elbow to her wrist.

Lifting the fingers protruding from her injured arm's cast dressing, he kissed them one by one.

"There's so much I want to do with you, Chloe." Her cheeks reddened at the implication. Laughing huskily, he tossed back his head. Once again, he curled his arm around her and gazed into her green eyes. He tilted her chin in his hand and kissed her again. This was a new beginning for him. He had never intended on marrying, and yet when Chloe Tanner stepped into his life, she changed everything. For the first time he could remember, he no longer had the sense of restlessness, the need to search for something new. To his surprise—he felt whole.

"I want to take you swimming. I want to take you for a sleigh ride in the snow. I want you to take me for a wild ride in your curricle. I'd like to play poker with you. I'd like to go to Paris with you…"

"Yes, yes."

"I want to share a glass of whiskey with you before a warm fire at night. But most of all, I'd like to wake up with you every morning in the same bed…"

"Yes," she answered breathlessly, "but for now, can you settle for just kissing me?"

"No, I mean, yes." He hastened to correct, taking her in his arms again.

****

Yes, the Angel's knew what they were about. How else to explain that the very person I chose to teach me what making love was all about—ended up teaching me about love itself. Chloe ran her fingers down his cheek, gliding her thumb across Pen's mustache as they continued to study each other. He reached up and captured her hand turning it over then pressed soft kisses to her pulse in a slow march up her bare arm.

"Something just dawned on me." She pulled her hand away.

Frowning at her rebuff, he waited her out.

"I have no one to give me away."

"When in your life, Chloe Tanner have you ever depended on a man for anything you wanted to do?" He laughed rolling his eyes upward. "We can elope if you wish. It's up to you. I am happy to marry you any way you'd like. As long as you don't wait too long. These intervals you give me between lovemaking are excruciatingly cruel."

"Pshaw. You are so pitiful, Pen Kittrell. Do you feel so mistreated?"

"Yes. And something's going to have to be done about that."

One by one, hard drops of rain pelted the tin rooftop. A consistent rhythm turned into a deluge within minutes, pulsating drumming sounds all around them. Water gushed from overflowing gutters and waterspouts, splashing into mud puddles on the grounds. Cheers and laughter whooping from the stable yard and distillery reverberated from excited voices, welcoming the downpour.

Chloe smiled, returning Pen's embrace with fervor, abandoning any attempt to keep his lovemaking to a moderate intensity.

Epilogue

May 1894

Pen walked from the stable area with Milo Knox. Breezes from the west rustled the last of spring's dogwood blooms, as the two ambled over to the corral fence to watch the new filly frisk about.

"What's this rumor I heard concerning you thinking about retiring?"

"Exactly that," he said spitting to the side, "a rumor. I got to ensure the next generation of Tanners knows the whiskey business from the ground up." He gave a nod to five-year-old Dillon Tanner, cantering around the paddock on a new roan pony.

"Good to hear."

"And what did the two of you decide?" Milo asked, pulling down the brim of his hat to watch the very expectant Mrs. Kittrell waddle up to them after kissing her mother goodbye following their Sunday visit.

"Well, we decided"—with a heavy emphasis on "we"—"we decided if it's a boy, he'll apprentice with me and one day run Kittrell's. And if it's a girl, she can come over here and train, then co-run Tanner's with her cousin. If she'd like to."

"If she's like her ma, she'd like that very much."

A word about the author…

As the daughter of a United States military officer, Joy Allyson grew up with a deep appreciation of history and a love of travel. A teacher by training, she always preferred reading historical romance to pedagogy. Joy believes the best romances are the ones you want to read over and over again.

She resides among the beautiful hills of Tennessee with her husband and near her two daughters and six grandchildren. She is a member of Romance Writers of America and Music City Writers. *Whiskey Love* is her debut novel.

Visit her at:
www.JoyAllyson.com

Thank you for purchasing
this publication of The Wild Rose Press, Inc.

For questions or more information
contact us at
info@thewildrosepress.com.

The Wild Rose Press, Inc.